"I would never hurt you."

"I know, Ian." Agnes's voice sounded raspy.

She bit her bottom lip to steady her trembling jaw, a tear slipping over her lower lashes and trailing down her cheek.

Ian crushed her to his chest. "Why didn't you come to me? I would have protected you."

She should move away. But, for that moment, she just wanted the strength of his embrace, and to rest her ear against his chest and listen to his beating heart.

Ian pulled back and cradled her face with both hands, his fingers threading in her hair. He kept his gaze steady with hers. "You are safe with me."

As his words soaked in, Agnes searched his face and cupped his jaw. "I know."

He placed his hands on her shoulders. His questioning eyes searched her face. "Red—"

She pressed a finger against his lips. "You're my protector, Ian. I feel safe here because of you."

Books by Lisa Jordan

Love Inspired

Lakeside Reunion
Lakeside Family
Lakeside Sweethearts

LISA JORDAN

has been writing for over a decade, taking a hiatus to earn her degree in early childhood education. By day, she operates an in-home family child-care business. By night, she writes contemporary Christian romances. Being a wife to her real-life hero and mother to two young adult men overflow her cup of blessings. In her spare time, she loves reading, knitting and hanging out with family and friends. Learn more about her at www.lisajordanbooks.com.

Lakeside Sweethearts

Lisa Jordan

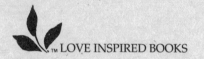 ™ LOVE INSPIRED BOOKS

ISBN-13: 978-0-373-87893-2

LAKESIDE SWEETHEARTS

Copyright © 2014 by Lisa Jordan

www.Harlequin.com

Printed in U.S.A.

He has made everything beautiful in its time. He has also set eternity in the hearts of men; yet they cannot fathom what God has done from beginning to end.
—*Ecclesiastes* 3:11

To Dr. Reba J. Hoffman, who inspired Agnes's character. You, my friend, are amazing. Thank you for your prayers, wisdom and encouragement. May your Road to Freedom impact others as much as you've impacted me.

To Dianne Sherman, whose passion and vision for the House of Hope ministry inspired this story. May God bless your ministry and the women in a way that leaves you breathless.

Acknowledgments

Susan May Warren, Rachel Hauck, Michelle Lim, Beth Vogt, Reba J. Hoffman, Edie Melson, Melissa Tagg, Alena Tauriainen, Roxanne Sherwood Gray, Sue Nebbe, Carolyn Vibbert & Amanda W.—thank you for your brainstorming, additional sets of eyes and feedback that helped to make this a stronger story.

Rachel Hauck & Lindsay Harrel— thank you for sharing your love stories as I strived to create the romance between Ian and Agnes.

Jude Urbanski—for sharing your story of how God triumphed through tragedy. Bill Giovanetti—for helping me to create Agnes's car trouble. R. Herrick, the Honorable Maureen Skerda, Reba J. Hoffman, Patrick Jordan and Jessica Koschnitzky—for information about the Pennsylvania Motor Vehicle Code, prison system, sentencing and parole information. Any mistakes are mine.

Melissa Endlich & Giselle Regus—my two incredible editors whose encouragement and revision notes challenged me to write the best story possible. Thank you to the rest of the Love Inspired team who had a hand in bringing my book to print.

Rachelle Gardner—my fairy godmother agent who tied the knot and encouraged me to hold on when my rope unraveled unexpectedly.

Patrick, Scott & Mitchell—your constant encouragement helps me to keep living the dream. I love you forever.

Most importantly, thank you, God, for loving me unconditionally in spite of my flaws and scars.

Chapter One

Red had to say yes. Restoring his family depended on it.

Ian James opened the door to Cuppa Josie's and entered Shelby Lake's finest coffeehouse, ushering the sun-soaked May breeze in with him. The wind ruffled the edges of the *Shelby Lake Gazette* splayed across the large storefront window counter. As he closed the door, the tattered bells rattled against the glass.

He slid off his sunglasses and slipped them in the breast pocket of his untucked button-down shirt, giving his eyes a minute to adjust to the abrupt change in lighting.

Today's special blend—crème brûlée according to the sign on the front door—mingled with the spicy aroma of Josie Brennan's signature white chicken chili, causing his stomach to grumble. The Saturday special on the chalkboard easel near the register boasted chocolate macadamia nut brownies as the dessert of the day.

Once he finished talking with Red, he'd grab lunch before heading back to the insurance office to go over a couple of claims with Dad. Then he needed to head out to Carl Winston's place to determine the extent of his recent garage fire.

Being a claims adjuster might not be a glamorous job or his dream career, but he liked helping people get what they needed.

Rustling newspapers, ringing cell phones and the buzz of conversations couldn't drown out Red's laughter that touched his ears before she appeared from the side dining room.

Ian swallowed back the knot in his throat that always seemed to form every time he saw her.

Agnes Kingsley, his best friend since her family moved next door from Texas to Shelby Lake about twenty-five years ago, had captured her ginger-colored hair in a ponytail that did little to keep a few curls from escaping and spiraling around her face.

The Cuppa Josie's apron tied twice around her narrow waist failed to hide her long legs and the slight curve of her hips. Large hoop earrings dangled from her ears.

Their first meeting was imprinted in his memory—she was ten and he was twelve. The pop fly he'd missed had rolled into her yard next door. She'd stepped from behind her family's moving van cradling the baseball between two fingers and her thumb. She'd smiled, her crazy mop of ginger hair askew. When she refused to give her name, he dubbed her "Red," and the rest was history.

The baby she cradled in her arms released a wail that jerked Ian back to the present. Red patted his back while talking to Lindsey Chase, Josie Brennan's stepsister.

Lindsey tucked a blond strand of hair behind her ear and touched her son's pajama-covered leg. "You'd make a great mom someday, Agnes."

A shadow flickered across her eyes. "As much as I love the little darlings, being a mama isn't going to happen."

"You say that now, but some guy will turn your head,

and then you'll be holding your own little one before you know it."

Despite Red's laughter, he recognized the hollow tone. And when she turned on the Texas charm, he knew to watch out...or rescue her, depending on her target.

He skirted past the couch in front of the unlit fireplace where some dude wearing headphones tapped his pencil against his laptop to the beat of his music. Winding through the square tables filled with the lunch crowd, Ian reached Lindsey and Red.

He caressed the newborn's soft head. "Hey, Linds. Congrats on your little guy. Sorry to interrupt, but can I steal Agnes from you?" Without waiting for her response, he touched Red's elbow. "You got a second? I need to talk to you about something."

"Sure." She breathed in the infant's scent once more, then handed him back to Lindsey. "Thanks for stopping in, Linds. Bring him back so I can hug his sweet little neck again."

To be that baby's neck...

Turning her attention to Ian, she nodded toward the side dining room. "Mind if we talk in there? I need to finish setting up for a private luncheon. Abby can handle the register."

Ian glanced at the seventeen-year-old flirting at the coffee counter with one of the Shelby Lake High football players. Yeah, she had it covered. He shook his head and followed Red into the side dining room. He half closed the door for a little privacy. "You okay?"

She smiled wide. "Just dandy. Why wouldn't I be?"

He leaned against the wall and shoved his hands in his pockets. "Maybe because of your Texas charm? Or maybe the fact that you won't look at me? Or maybe the way your hand is trembling while you fold that napkin?"

She tossed the yellow napkin on the table and crossed her arms over her chest. "I'm just fine, Ian James. Either speak your piece or leave me be. I have work to do."

Ian rounded the long tables covered with white cloths and cupped her chin, lifting her face to meet his gaze. Sadness fringed her electric blue eyes. He caressed her cheekbone with his thumb. "You're better than fine, Red. I've been telling you that for years. But something upset you. What's going on in that stubborn head of yours?"

Red's shoulders slumped as she pressed her forehead against his chest. He wrapped his arms around her, breathing in the scent of her expensive perfume—the one gift he bought her every year because she refused to spend the money on herself.

"Why does everyone think a woman needs a husband and a baby to be complete? There's more to life than being some guy's doormat and changing diapers."

"Being married doesn't make you a doormat. Besides, I'm sure Lindsey meant nothing by her comment. You're just a natural when it comes to kids. From teaching your teen Sunday school class and overseeing the nursery—it's obvious that you love them."

"But not every woman can—I mean—wants to raise a passel of babies." She pushed him away and waved her hands, as if dispersing with that conversation. "What are you doing here anyway? Weren't you supposed to go to some craft fair with Emily?"

After being best friends with Red for so long, he knew when to back off.

He didn't really want to talk about his change in plans for the day either, but Red needed to hear the news from him instead of from some customers' gossiping.

"Yeah, about that…" Sighing, he pulled out a chair,

dropped on it and scrubbed a hand over his face. "Em broke up with me last night."

Red placed her hand on his shoulder. "I'm so sorry. Why?"

"She feels I don't devote enough time to her."

"She's right—you don't. But it's really not your fault. You can't work her banker's hours. You're required to be in the field when most people are eating dinner or chilling out on weekends. Plus, with running your nephew to practice and feeding your caffeine addiction here, I'm surprised you had time to take her to dinner."

"Thanks, friend. Whose side are you on?" And his coffee addiction happened so he could see Red.

"Get real, Ian. A woman wants to know she's valued in a guy's life. Even with your demanding job, you could make more time to be with her if you really wanted."

He shrugged and leaned back in the chair. "You're right."

"Well, maybe its good you found out now."

"Yeah, especially now."

"Why do you say that?"

"Well, for one thing, I don't see myself spending the rest of my life with her."

"Why not?"

She's not you.

But he couldn't say it.

"You're almost thirty-eight, Ian. You've wanted a wife and family for a while. Maybe it's time to think about settling down."

His conversation with Emily last night made him realize he didn't want to just date for the sake of going out. He wanted the one woman who'd stolen his heart a couple of decades ago.

He wanted Red.

And now he was determined to prove they belonged together.

"You should take your own advice," he said.

"Tried that, remember? Apparently, I'm not enough to make a man happy."

"You need the right man, Red. Your ex was a jerk, who couldn't see what a great woman he had." Ian stood and reached for Red's hand. He ran a thumb over her soft skin.

Red glanced at her hand, then shot him a puzzled look before pulling her fingers away gently. "We can talk more later, if you'd like, but I really need to finish setting up in here."

"That's not what I wanted to talk to you about anyway.... I got sidetracked. Can you spare a couple more minutes?"

"What's going on?"

Fifteen minutes ago, he had forced himself not to sprint down the street to share his news with her. Now his stomach knotted, and his throat felt as dry as day-old toast. "I just left Seaver Realty."

"Really?" Red leaned over the table to adjust the pink and yellow roses in floral teacups, her ponytail falling forward over her shoulder. "What for? Planning to move out of your parents' basement?"

"Nah, haven't gotten that lucky yet. I'll be there to lend a hand until Zoe's released from prison and can care for Griffin on her own." He paused a minute to choose his next words carefully. "The board voted on a place for Agape House. Mom signed the final paperwork today."

"That was fast." She smacked him with a napkin. "Why didn't you say anything, Ian James?"

"Well, it happened rather quickly. Once Mom learned my sister's parole hearing would be in August, she's been pushing them to agree on one of the houses Alec's already shown them. So they made a decision last night and signed papers today. Thanks to community donations and corporate sponsorships, the house has been paid in full."

"That's great, Ian." Red did a little dance and opened her arms. "Get over here so I can hug your neck. I know how important this is to your family."

He gathered her against his chest again, her hair whispering against his chin. Could she feel his heart hammering against his ribs? "Yeah, thanks. Mom hopes the parole board will be in favor of releasing Zoe in August if she has a transitional home to go to."

"Doesn't give you much time to get a house ready."

"Exactly. Which brings me to my next thing—the board chose an estate that's structurally sound but needs some work—inside and out. Plus, Mom's talking repainting, new curtains…stuff like that."

"Makes sense. A fresh coat of paint covers a multitude of scars." Red walked to the window and adjusted the blinds to allow light to pour across the chocolate-brown carpet.

Ian shoved his hands in the front pockets of his faded jeans. "She wants to know if you're interested in the job."

"But I have a job." She reached for a yellow napkin and folded it into a fan before setting it on one of the white dinner plates.

"This is part-time and temporary. You have great budgeting and organizational skills to coordinate the volunteers helping with cleaning and painting. There's a stipend set aside for whoever takes the job." Ian reached for one of the napkins and copied Red's folding. "Mom loves your repurposed furniture. She wants to buy pieces for Agape House and will showcase your work to help spread the word about your business."

Agnes pressed a hand to her chest. "Ian, I don't know what to say. It's so generous. I love working for Josie and

Nick, but opening Tattered Daisies Furniture has been a dream for so long."

"This takes you one step closer to having your own storefront. Say yes."

"Where's the place?" She handed him a pitcher of ice water and pointed to the place settings across from her. "Please fill those glasses."

This was the tough part.

"Well, that's the thing." Ice clinked against the clear glass as he filled the goblets halfway with water. He set the pitcher on the table and leaned forward, bracing his hands on the table. "It's the old Miller estate on Liberty Street."

Her head jerked up, causing her to slosh water over the edge of the goblet she had been filling. "Wait a minute… what?"

He snatched napkins off the table behind him and thrust them at her. Maybe she hadn't heard him. "The Miller estate on Liberty. You know that gray house with the black shutters?"

"I heard you, idiot." She slid the flower arrangements out of the way and pressed the napkins onto the spreading water. Flatware clattered against the plates as she cleared the table.

"Hey, what's up with that?"

Shaking out a clean cloth, she glared at him as if she wanted to dump the water over his head. "You're acting about as dense as a fence post. You asked me to help knowing how much I despise that place."

He rubbed a damp hand over his face. He had expected her to be less than thrilled once she found out, but he had nothing to do with the building choice.

"It's been over five years. I just thought—"

"Ian, I'd do almost anything for you…for your family. Especially after what your daddy did for mine all those years ago. But I can't do this. And you of all people shouldn't be asking me." She bundled the damp tablecloth and wet napkins into a ball.

"Listen—"

She held up a hand. "No, you listen. I said I'd never step foot in that wretched house again."

Ian rounded the table and stood in front of her. "I know your marriage to Bobby wasn't what you had envisioned, but he's not around anymore. You even went back to your maiden name. He has no hold on you."

She dropped her eyes to the wet fabric in her arms. "That house holds nothing but bad memories for me. I've spent the past five and a half years putting that decade of my life behind me."

"Have you?" He tipped her chin.

"Have I what?"

"Put it behind you? If so, then going back to that house wouldn't be a problem."

She pushed past him and headed for the door. "You have no idea."

He reached for her arm. "I can't do this alone."

"My head is ready to jump on board, but my heart… well, they're not on speaking terms at the moment. I know this is so important to all y'all. Just once I wish God would take a shine to answering one of my dreams."

The longing in her voice needled his heart. "God has a dream bigger than your own, Red. What He gives you will be greater than anything you've ever imagined."

"Not for a throwaway like me." The desolation on her face twisted his gut. "You're hoping to restore that place into a house of hope, but don't y'all see? It will never be anything but a house of pain."

She pushed past him and hurried into the main dining

room. The lingering scent of her perfume wasn't strong enough to mask the defeat that settled over his shoulders.

He had been so sure she'd say yes. But now he needed to find another way to convince her to agree—for all of their sakes.

He wanted her help with Agape House, but not just for restoring his family. More than that, he wanted to restore her heart and prove she was worthy of being loved.

If she were a real friend, she'd shove her regrets and bad memories into the past where they belonged and help Ian. As her family's dearest friends, they'd drop everything if the roles were reversed.

So why couldn't she do it?

Agnes shoved the tablecloths into the washer and slammed the lid, trying to blot Ian's pleading eyes from her memory.

Being in that house would release the ghosts she'd managed to imprison so she'd have some semblance of a normal life.

Saying no was her only option.

Agnes returned to the kitchen to find it empty, but a light glowed from under Josie's closed office door. Probably needed a few minutes with her feet up.

Josie's pregnancy with Noah, her eleven-month-old, had been a piece of cake. With this new pregnancy, she dealt with a lot of morning sickness…or as she called it—all day sickness.

Agnes tried to convince her to go home, but she insisted on helping with the luncheon.

Agnes opened the stainless steel industrial refrigerator and reached for the glass bowl of mixed greens. Balancing the covered bowl against her chest, she grabbed the stack of salad plates chilling on the top shelf and closed the door with her foot. She set everything on the stainless counter, then washed her hands.

Not even the scent of lemon meringue pie baking in the oven could add sweetness to her sour mood.

The kitchen door swung open, and Hannah, Josie and Nick's twelve-year-old daughter, bounced into the kitchen, wearing brown leggings, a blue fitted T-shirt that matched the rest of the Cuppa Josie's staff and a striped Cuppa Josie's apron.

Although she was too young to work, Hannah liked to volunteer and help when Josie had private parties in the side dining room.

"I'm here to help, Aggie. Tell me what you need." Hannah rested an elbow on the counter and snatched a tomato out of the salad Agnes pulled from the fridge.

Agnes tapped her on the nose. "Thanks, Sugar Pie."

Two years ago, Nick had donated his bone marrow to knock the leukemia from her body. Now Hannah thrived with color restored back in her cheeks. A miniature clone of Josie, but with her daddy's eyes and nose, Hannah had chin-length cocoa-colored hair, held back with a flowered headband. Almost as tall as Josie now, she had a sweet spirit that touched everyone she met.

"Have you seen Mom?"

"Her office light is on. She may be taking a breather for a minute."

Agnes nodded toward the glass plates she had pulled from the fridge. "Please take those to the side dining room and set them on the buffet table. The coffee and tea are already on the beverage table, but you could put out some lemonade. I'll be in with the salad as soon as I add the cranberries and almonds."

Hannah reached for the plates and pushed through the door.

Josie chose that moment to return to the kitchen, refastening her hair into a messy bun. A blue Cuppa Josie's apron tied at her waist emphasized her expanding belly. "Sorry for ditching you. One of the coffee suppliers called to confirm a new shipment."

"Everything straightened out?"

"Yes, I will be able to use my superpowers to continue to caffeinate the world." She stifled a yawn. Dark circles gathered under her brown eyes, highlighting her pale skin.

Agnes opened the bag of dried cranberries and poured them into the salad. "Sugar Pie, why don't you let me handle this luncheon, and you put your feet up?"

"Agnes, this isn't 1950. I've been pregnant before. I can handle it." Josie smiled as she reached for pot holders to pull the pie out of the oven.

"You've been working since six this morning. Surely you could use a break."

"I'll leave as soon as the luncheon is done. I promise. Hannah's here to help. Nick took Noah to Dad and Gracie's. So we're all good." Josie pulled eggs from the fridge and set them on the counter next to her KitchenAid mixer.

Agnes waved the salad tongs at her. "I'm sticking you to it."

With one hand bracing the counter and the other folded on her hip, Josie gave Agnes a pointed look. "So, are you going to tell me what's going on?"

No use in pretending she didn't know what Josie was talking about. No matter how wide her smile, Josie could always pinpoint when Agnes had something stuck in her craw. She stared at the salad, trying to figure out what to say. "I'm a fool. And a rotten friend."

"I doubt that." Josie pulled over a stool and patted the top. "Have a seat and tell me what happened."

"Men can be so clueless."

"Uh, yeah, hello—I married one. Nick's great, but he has his moments. What's up?"

Agnes recapped her earlier conversation with Ian, including his breakup with Emily.

"Sweetie, you're hardly a terrible friend. Does Ian know why the house holds such bad memories for you?"

"He knows about Bobby's cheating and gambling, and the fall, but the rest is too painful to talk about."

Her ex-husband's name sent a shudder through her. Permanent gouges scarred her heart, thanks to her ex's straying.

The first time it had happened, she'd been hoodwinked by his tearful promises that proved to be as empty as his bank account. The second time she left, he managed to lure her home after a week. Again more empty promises. The third…well, that was for good.

His lies and cheating destroyed more than her credit rating and their marriage that night.

"I didn't mean to bring up a sensitive subject."

"No worries. Like Ian said—it's in the past." Agnes slid off the stool. "Let's get the food set out so you can get out of here."

"Just a second." Josie opened the carton and reached for an egg but made no move to break it. "Now that Ian and Emily aren't together, what are you going to do?"

"Do?"

"Now's your chance, Agnes."

"Chance for what?"

"To let Ian know how you really feel about him."

"Ian is my best friend. We need to leave it at that."

"Why?"

"Why? Because I said so…that's why."

"Oh, good answer." Josie cracked the egg on the edge

of her mixer bowl. "Life is passing you by, Agnes. You spend your time serving and caring about others. It's time to knock down those walls around your heart and go after what you truly want."

"If only it were that simple. Years ago, I let Ian know how I felt before I went off to college in Texas. Ian said he didn't want me to feel tied down in a long distance relationship. Then, over Christmas break, he mentioned he had started seeing someone at school. Bobby asked me out, and I guess the rest is history."

"You quit school after your freshman year to get married, right? That was almost twenty years ago. That boy is a *man* who drools over you like a morning pastry. Maybe working together on Agape House would be a great way to see if there could be more than friendship between you two."

"Ian deserves the family I can't give him. Besides, I can't risk our friendship. Not again. If something destroyed that, then I'd have nothing. My heart couldn't bear that."

"I've seen the way he looks at you, Agnes. Maybe it's time you threw caution to the wind and took a chance before someone else snatches him up."

"Maybe someone should. At least he could have the future he's always wanted."

With Josie's words ringing in her ears, Agnes fixed a smile in place and reached for the salad. She walked into the side dining room and set the bowl of mixed greens on the buffet table. Hannah, bless her heart, brought in pitchers of lemonade. Josie followed with a platter of chicken salad croissants and a glass pedestal bowl of cut fresh fruit.

Nancy, the hostess of the luncheon, arrived. While

Josie spoke to her about the food, Agnes retreated to the kitchen.

Hannah poked her head inside the kitchen door. "Mr. Higby's looking for you."

"Clarence? My landlord?"

She nodded, then held the door open wide enough for Agnes to see the burly man drumming his fingers on the counter by the register.

Agnes followed Hannah into the main dining room. "Hey, Clarence."

Clarence Higby ran a finger between the collar of his flannel shirt and his doughy neck. He gripped a white envelope in his other hand. "Agnes, do you have a moment?"

"Sure, what's up?"

Clarence always reminded her of Papa Bear from *Goldilocks*—brawny with whiskered jowls…and the red suspenders he wore with his cuffed jeans.

"I planned to come by later this afternoon, but when Eliza mentioned her ladies' thing was here, I wanted you to hear this from me and not overheard from a bunch of hens."

Agnes didn't like the direction this conversation was going.

He thrust the envelope at her.

She took it, noticed her name scrawled on the front, then looked at him. "What's this?"

"The letter says it so much better. Eliza typed it. She's the one who's good with words." He heaved a sigh, then scraped his sausage fingers through his thinning salt-and-pepper hair. "Eliza and me…well, we've decided to move to Arizona."

"Arizona? You've lived in Shelby Lake your entire life."

"Our daughter Jocelyn is pregnant." Clarence beamed like a proud grandpa-to-be. "After she lost the first two, she and Aaron wanted to wait until she was out of the danger zone to announce this pregnancy."

She forced her lips into a smile, hoping to project joy she didn't feel. "Well, that's fantastic. When's the baby due?"

"November—around Thanksgiving."

"Truly something to be thankful for."

"Eliza and I don't want our grandchild to grow up without seeing us but a few times a year, so we've decided to move to Arizona before the baby's born. The air is better for Eliza's arthritis, too. You know how these damp seasons make her ache so."

"But…"

Of course she understood they wanted to be with their family, but what about her apartment?

As if reading her thoughts, Clarence laid a beefy hand on her shoulder. "We sold the building. Yesterday. That's what I wanted you to hear from me."

His news pushed her stomach into a free fall to her toes. "I didn't even know it was for sale. How long do I have to look for a new place?"

"Thirty days."

Air whooshed out of her lungs as if someone had stepped on her ribs. She slumped against the counter, crushing the envelope in her fist.

Thirty days?

Where was she going to find an affordable place in such a short time?

He mentioned selling her apartment building, but what about their cottage?

"Are you planning to rent out your cottage?"

He shook his head. "Nope. We're listing it with Seaver Realty on Monday."

She loved the lakefront peach-colored cottage with its white trim and wide front porch. Flower beds skirted the perimeter of the house, and a large backyard meant for barbecues and kickball games overlooked the lake. A white picket fence hemmed it all in.

The kind of place she always dreamed about, complete with rocking chairs on the front porch so she could grow old with someone who found her worth loving.

An image of Ian with silver hair flashed through her mind.

Refusing to give up on owning a place to call home, Agnes continued to put away money. Someday the right house would be available. For now, she'd keep saving her pennies. Unless…

No, that was crazy thinking.

She could barely make her rent each month, thanks to paying off her ex's gambling debts. The cottage was going to be way out of her price range.

But Ian's request to help with Agape House came to mind.

If she could push to sell her restored furniture, then maybe, just maybe, she could manage a down payment and get a loan for the mortgage.

Heart hammering against her ribs, she turned to her landlord and blurted, "Clarence, would you and Eliza consider selling the cottage to me?"

He scrubbed a hand over his whiskers. "Now, there's an idea. You've been a great tenant. Let me talk it over with her this afternoon. I'll give you a call this evening."

"Sure, that's fine. I won't be home for a bit anyway."

After Clarence left, Agnes checked on the ladies, then hurried to the kitchen. Pulling her cell phone from her pocket, she stared at the screen saver of her and Ian as teenagers, grinning as they hoisted the Golden Paddle Award in the air.

Good times.

They made a great team. In more ways than one.

Could she do this? Could her heart handle the risk?

No going back if she said yes.

If she wanted to put the past behind her to face a new future, she had to take the first step. And if she wanted to buy the cottage, she needed the extra income to help with the down payment.

Her thumb hovered over the two on her speed dial. She pressed it and held her breath until Ian's deep voice answered. She released her breath. "Hey, it's me. I'll do it."

No going back now.

Now she needed to find the courage to put the past to rest.

Chapter Two

When she walked out that door over five years ago, Agnes never thought she'd cross the threshold again.

But here she was.

The chipped gray paint and sagging black shutters of the house on the corner lot held nothing but echoes of angry voices and empty promises.

A sold placard nested on top of the sun-bleached for sale sign swinging in the wind, the rusting chain creaking with each movement.

If she focused on the physical attributes of the house, then maybe she could ignore memories that threatened to resurface simply by walking through the door.

"I can't believe you talked me into coming here today. I haven't even changed from work." Agnes marched up the sidewalk behind Ian, her legs fighting not to turn and run with each step closer to the door.

"No time like the present." Glancing over his shoulder, he flashed a smile that always made her insides twirl.

Dressed in faded jeans with a threadbare hole in the thigh, a gray T-shirt advertising James & Son Insurance and leather deck shoes that had seen better days, Ian inserted the key and unlocked the door, but didn't push it open. Keeping one hand clenched on the doorknob, he dragged his fingers through his hair, tousling his sandy-brown curls in need of a cut.

His forget-me-not-blue eyes pleaded with her. "Listen, Red, if you're not ready, then Mom and I will find someone else to help."

She tightened her hand around her purse strap, praying this morning's breakfast of tea and toast didn't cause a revolt.

Why did it have to be this house?

A gentle breeze stirred the curls of her ponytail, brushing them against her jaw. She closed her eyes and lifted her face to the warming rays of sunshine.

"Ready?"

She looked at him, pulling energy from the compassion warming his eyes. "Let's get this over with."

Ian opened the door and stepped back, ushering her to step inside.

Agnes stepped on the black welcome mat covering the stoop and tried not to scoff at the irony. She hadn't felt welcome here in a long time. Steeling her spine, she strode inside and sucked in a breath.

A musty smell tinged with the faint odor of stale cigarette smoke tangled with the fresh air coming in through the front door. Pushing her white sunglasses on top of her head, she waited a moment for her eyes to adjust. "How long has this place been empty?"

"I think Alec said a year or so. Cliff Miller died last spring, and the family's been trying to sell it since then."

Flat beige walls pocked with nail holes added an air of despair to the barren room. Water stains marked the yellowed ceiling. A ratty calico rug covered a large portion of the parched wooden floor. A wide archway led into a smaller room.

What happened to the cream-colored walls and the gleaming wooden floor?

She had taken pride in making the house cozy and keeping it clean, even with their limited budget.

The thirsty floorboards creaked beneath their feet as they moved from the living room into the dining room.

Memories of a different life drifted up from behind every crack and crevice, threatening to buckle her knees.

Love had been a constant in the beginning months of her marriage to Bobby Levine, but those rose-colored glasses cracked before their second anniversary when she learned about his first affair. The beginning of broken promises, pleas for second chances...and thirds.

She'd spent ten years in this house until... Her eyes skimmed the staircase hugging the left wall.... No, she definitely wasn't going there. She shifted her gaze and hurried through the archway into the kitchen.

Bracing her hands against the stained porcelain sink, she forced the shudder in her chest to calm. She stared out the cracked window to the backyard at the mangled rosebush and neglected flower beds.

"Red?"

She turned and nearly bumped into Ian.

Agnes ran a trembling hand along the counter dulled by decades of use. She cleared her throat and squared her shoulders. "Sorry, I kind of just took off."

"No need for apologies."

The yellowed floral-printed wallpaper curled at the corners. She pressed the brittle paper back in place, but the moment she let go, the edges pulled away from the wall. She knew that feeling of continuing to hold on, wondering if hope had forgotten her.

"If your mama had chosen a different house, I'd have the first coat of paint on the walls already."

"We can't deal in 'if only.'" He tucked a stray curl behind her ear, his hand lingering on her hair. "Given the chance, this house—and the women in it—can be redeemed. Sometimes it takes peeling away the layers to find the promise for the future. But if you don't think you can do it—"

"I said I'd do it." She stepped away from his touch and waved a hand over the kitchen. "It's just a little tough being here again. That was a painful time in my life."

"I know. If I could turn back time, I'd object to you marrying that jerk." The muscle in his jaw twitched, and his hand balled into a fist.

"You had the chance. Why didn't you?" The words slipped over her lips before she had time to think about what she had just said.

He turned away. "You chose him. I couldn't stand in the way of your happiness."

Angry tears threatened. Her happiness? The only man she had wanted to stand beside her at the altar saw her as a buddy, a pal.

No, she hadn't chosen. She'd settled.

"I asked you if there was any reason why I shouldn't marry Bobby. You said no."

"I was your friend, Red. I couldn't stand in the way of your future."

She scoffed and shook her head.

Friend.

Right.

He faced her again, a scowl scrunching his eyebrows. "That creep and this house have drained you emotionally. Now it's time for healing. Learn to let go and forgive. Leave the past where it belongs and focus on your future, Red."

"I don't know what the future holds." She wrapped her arms around her middle.

"But God does. I'm here for you, too."

"You're a good friend, Ian. The best a girl could have."

He shook his head and scrubbed a hand over his face. "Friend. Yes, seems to be my lot in life."

"What do you mean by that?"

"Nothing. I'm proud of you, Red. Just so you know that…. You said you'd never step foot in this house again, and look where you are now."

"Yeah, well, you were pretty convincing."

He glanced at his watch. "I have an appointment soon, but first I want to check upstairs." He grabbed her hand and dragged her out of the kitchen and into the dining room toward the steps.

Agnes tried to pull her hand from his grasp. "Wait, where are you taking me?"

He released her hand and gripped the nicked banister. "Just upstairs."

Agnes's eyes studied each step until they reached the top. She lifted a foot onto the first step. Her breath choked in her throat.

Ian scowled and said something, but the roaring in her ears drowned out his words.

Yelling. Accusations. Pleas. Broken promises jostled at a locked door in the back of her mind. Feeling that first step beneath her foot pried that door of memories loose, exposing past aches.

Her heart raced as her breathing quickened. She squeezed her eyes shut. She watched herself reliving the fall—every bone and muscle knocking off the steps—until she landed in a crumbled heap at the bottom, aching for what she had lost.

Those bones healed and the bruises faded, but Bobby's role in her accidental fall tore away a part of her that could never be put back together.

Agnes wrapped her arms around her stomach. *God, please...make it stop.*

She shook her head, tears flooding her eyes. "I can't go up there. I just can't."

Turning, she fled to the front door, wrenched it open and stumbled into the sunshine. Without checking to see if Ian followed her, she hurried down the sidewalk past his Ford Escape.

Ian wanted this house to bring his family back together, but how could they find hope when all she felt was pain?

As long as he lived, he'd never forget the look of torture that contorted Red's pale face as she stared up at him from the bottom of the steps.

He wanted to gather her to his chest and protect her from her past. But that was impossible. All he could do now was help her to face it in order to heal and have the life God desired for her.

Palming the warm pizza on one hand, Ian rapped his knuckles against Red's front door, praying she didn't slam it back in his face.

A moment later, she opened it, giving him a wary smile. "If you're fixing to change my mind about going upstairs, it's not going to happen."

"Of course not." Ian held out the large red and white box. "Pizza offering?"

"Come in. It's not polite for a girl to leave a guy standing on her front step."

"Especially when he's holding her favorite pizza."

"Especially then." She flashed a quick smile, giving him a glimpse of the spunky Red he knew and loved.

The exterior of Red's brick apartment building lacked character, but her place exploded with color. Cream-colored walls, an orange couch, a bluish-green printed chair with matching ottoman, sheer blue curtains hanging from tree branch curtain rods that had been pushed back to allow the sunshine to spill across the hardwood floor. White daisies in a yellow pitcher sat on a wicker and glass coffee table. And plants in colored pots sat all over the place.

She had exchanged her work clothes for cutoff denim shorts that showcased her bare legs and a blue Lone Star State T-shirt. Red pulled the ponytail holder out of her hair and tossed it in a pottery bowl on the end table. She fluffed her ginger curls around her face, then took the pizza from him.

Ian followed her through the living room into the kitchen.

She set the box on the table and pulled two red stoneware plates from the cupboard. Ian opened the lid, releasing scents of yeast, tomatoes and oregano.

She peeked over his shoulder, her hair brushing against his cheek. "You got pineapple and ham. My favorite."

"Of course." He took a step back to keep from winding one of those curls around his finger. Hands off. He was her friend. "You want to tell me why you hightailed it out of there so quickly?"

She set the plates on the table and turned away to open a drawer. Grabbing two forks, she looked at him, her eyes shrouded with pain.

She thrust the utensils sat him, then turned and gripped the edge of the sink. "Even after all this time, the stairs…well, they're a visual reminder of the fall and what I lost that night. I guess I kind of freaked out. Sorry. Anyway, let's eat before this pizza gets cold."

She flashed him another quick smile, but this one did little to extinguish the torment in her eyes. She reached into the box to lift out a slice of pizza. Wrapping the melted cheese strings around her finger, she nodded toward the living room. "Let's eat in there. Grab us a couple of Cokes, will you?"

Leaning against the sink, he watched her leave and ground his teeth together. He wanted to kick himself for pushing her into going to the house when she wasn't ready.

Way to go, dude.

He grabbed their drinks, then closed the refrigerator door with his hip. Snatching his plate, he headed for the living room.

Red set her plate on the coffee table and pushed the pitcher out of the way to make room for his before sitting on the couch.

Once Ian settled on the cushion next to her, he reached for her hand. "Let's pray before I start eating like a heathen."

They bowed their heads while Ian blessed the food.

She echoed his "amen" and gave his hand a light squeeze, sending a shock of heat up his arm.

He pulled his fingers out of her grasp and reached for his pizza. "So, have you forgiven me yet?"

"There's nothing to forgive, Ian. You didn't do anything wrong. I was just…overwhelmed, I guess." She rested her head against the back of the couch, her hair fanning against a multicolored afghan.

He nudged her shoulder with his. "Still, if it's too much, we can find someone else to paint. You know what the rooms look like. Choosing colors and all that stuff with Mom won't be too bad, will it? Then volunteers can handle the rest."

"No, I don't want you to do that." She shrugged, rubbing her hands on her thighs. "The Lord and me...we'll get it figured out."

"Maybe this is His way of saying it's time to move on...to something new."

"We'll see. Did I see you sneak in a Cuppa Josie's bag?"

"If I say yes, do you promise to keep me in the loop about how you're dealing with the house?"

"Depends on what's in the bag."

"Josie's chocolate macadamia nut brownies."

Agnes closed her eyes and groaned. "Guess I'll have to stick with one piece of pizza. I can't afford to buy new jeans."

"Believe me, Red. There's nothing wrong with your jeans." He threw his crust on his plate and wiped his fingers on a paper napkin.

"Ian, I'm in to help with the house. Just let me work at my own pace. I promise to have the job done by your mama's deadline."

"You bet. With your talents and my brawn..." He paused to flex his muscles. "We can whip that house into shape in time for Zoe to come home."

"When are you going to find time to remodel a house in a few short months? Your job keeps you going all over the county. And when you're not working, you're harassing me or hauling your nephew to practice."

"Nice to know you worry about me." He winked at her. He liked knowing she cared.

She bumped him with her shoulder. "Well, someone has to."

"I've wanted to fix houses since we took that mission trip over spring break in high school—you remember, when we helped that family fix their house after the hurricane? If I can help others, then I'll make the time to do it."

"You talked about my dreams, but when are you going to start living yours?"

"Being a claims adjuster is my job. Pursuing my passion of restoring houses feels a little out of reach. Opening Agape House and bringing Zoe home take priority. My dreams can wait once my family is restored."

"You're a good man, Ian, but what about starting your own family?"

"We talked about this, Red." He scoffed and shook his head. "My life is crazy. I don't have time right now. I didn't spend enough time with Emily, remember?"

Dating women who weren't Red didn't appeal to him. He needed to focus on convincing her he was the right man for her.

"You need some fun in your life."

"Yeah, well, that's going to have to wait." He stood and reached for his empty plate. "Sorry to eat and run, but I have to pick up Griffin from his buddy's house."

Red took his plate and set it on top of hers. "How's that cute little nephew of yours doing?"

"He'd hate hearing you calling him cute or little. Being eight is a big deal, you know. Counting down the days to when he turns nine, which is around the time Zoe should be home."

"He sure misses his mama."

"We all do. If I had taken her call that night, then Zoe would be raising her kid instead of Mom and Dad."

"You said we can't focus on the 'if onlys' in life. Zoe chose to drink and drive, resulting in the loss of someone's life. It's tragic, but that's not your burden to carry." Red squeezed his shoulder.

Her gentle touch sparked his skin through his shirt.

He reached for her hand and brushed a soft kiss across her fingers. "Says the queen burden carrier."

She pulled her hands away and fisted them under her arms. "Has your dad come around?"

Ian crossed to the door and gripped the doorknob. "Nope, still as stubborn as ever. Thank God he doesn't take out his anger at my sister on Griffin. He dotes on the kid."

"Maybe Agape House is what y'all need."

"I hope so, Red. At least for Griff's sake. I don't know how much more he can take. My sister's made plenty of poor choices. Her kid doesn't need to suffer because of them."

"The rest of her life will be shaped by those choices. You need to stop dwelling on the false guilt you carry and focus on supporting Zoe's fresh start and consider your own future."

Didn't she realize he couldn't consider his future without her in it?

Chapter Three

When Mama decided she was done celebrating birthdays because they made her feel old, Agnes figured she'd better make her last party a doozy, even if Mama grumbled about turning sixty.

Aqua, yellow and lime-green balloons tied to the cedar rails rimming Mama's back deck danced in the humid air. Streamers fluttered like kite tails. At least the rain held off, and the cloud cover kept the sun from baking the guests.

Agnes jammed the knife down the center of a buttercream-yellow rose, slid the piece of birthday cake onto a paper plate and handed it to Tyler Chase, Stephen and Lindsey's son.

"Thanks, Miss Agnes." He trotted off, trying to shove a forkful of cake in his mouth before skittering down the deck steps to the yard.

She started to call out for him to slow down, but Lindsey snatched him first.

Satisfied the child wasn't about to impale his tonsils, Agnes checked the pitchers of sweet tea and lemonade to make sure they were at least half-full.

Then she reached for her camera to snap a few more

pictures of guests sitting at the borrowed picnic tables covered in white tablecloths that dotted the backyard and of church friends gathered inside the gazebo Daddy had built for Mama as a twenty-fifth anniversary present.

Agnes zoomed in on Mama's group of Sunday school terrors kneeling on the stones ringing the handmade koi pond, harassing the fat orange fish darting under the floating lily pads.

Sitting in the shade with her friends, Mama seemed to be enjoying herself as they watched the couples from church play cornhole.

Agnes focused on Ian. Still dressed in his tan dress pants and white polo shirt from church, he juggled the four corn-filled bags. He stepped forward and tossed one of the bags into the cornhole board across the grass. His shirt stretched across his back. His muscled forearms rippled.

Agnes's face burned at the memory of his strong hands on her back when he hugged her.

Ian turned, filling her viewfinder with his wind-tossed hair and wide grin. She snapped as he winked and waved at her. Her heart somersaulted against her ribs.

Josie stepped through the sliding glass door onto the deck with a fresh carton of vanilla ice cream. She set it in a tub of ice next to the sundae fixings, then tossed the empty carton into the trash can at the bottom of the steps.

"With an arm like that, maybe you should be joining your hubby in tossing those corn bags."

"Nah, I couldn't show him up in front of his friends." Josie grabbed a strawberry from the watermelon fruit basket and leaned against the railing. "So, did you talk to your mom yet?"

Agnes reached for her camera again and focused on

Josie's expression as she smiled and reached for another berry. "Haven't had time. It's been a whirlwind weekend."

Agnes set the camera down and reached for her sweet tea, pressing the cool glass against her heated cheeks. "I'll talk to her after everyone leaves."

"Talk to who, darlin'?"

Hearing Mama's voice, Agnes stiffened. The woman had the stealth of a polecat. Agnes turned to find Mama climbing the deck stairs.

The wind ruffled the spiky points of Mama's short cap of snowy hair. Hours spent tending to her gardens this spring afforded a sun-kissed glow across her narrow face. Her white crocheted sweater over a peacock blue and lime-green printed dress shaved a decade off her years. Agnes hoped she would age as gracefully.

"I thought you were watching the cornhole game. Would you like more lemonade, or maybe another piece of cake?" Agnes asked her.

"Agnes Joy, what's going on?" Mama crossed her arms and raised her eyebrows.

Josie scooted along the deck railing toward the stairs and gestured she was going to the backyard.

Traitor.

Sighing, Agnes wiped her hands on the damp cloth on the edge of the table. Like a hound treeing a racoon, Mama wouldn't leave well enough alone until Agnes told her. "No need to worry, but my building's been sold. I have about a month to find a new place."

Mama pressed a hand to her chest and gripped the edge of the table. "Oh, my lands, that's absolutely perfect."

So much for Mama freaking out.

"What are you talking about?"

"The timing, darlin'."

"Perfect timing for what?"

"I was just telling the girls your memaw asked me to come back to Texas for the summer and help her rid up the house before she puts it up for sale. She wants to move into a condo for seniors. Less fuss."

"When was this? You hadn't said anything about it."

"I held off committing to the whole summer because I promised to help Charlotte with Agape House. Plus, I'd need someone to keep an eye on things." Mama waved a hand over the yard, then turned back to Agnes. "So this works out perfectly. We'll store your things in the garage, and you can stay here. Since you won't have to pay rent, you can save that money for the dream house you're always talking about."

Clarence and Eliza's cottage.

They'd agreed to sell her the house, but she hadn't had time to tell Mama all the particulars. Saving rent money and working at Agape House would help her to own the cottage a little sooner. So why wasn't she jumping on Mama's offer?

"I don't know, Mama. I'm a little old to be moving back home, don't you think?"

"Who said anything about moving back home? You'd be doing me a favor. Unless you'd rather not, of course…." Mama's not-so-innocent sidelong glance and words frosted Agnes with a layer of guilt as thick as the buttercream frosting on her birthday cake.

"Of course I want to help, Mama. But…"

So maybe Agnes didn't love the old brick building with its creaky pipes, temperamental heating and noisy neighbors, but the apartment had been hers to do as she pleased within the boundaries of her lease.

In less than a month, though, she'd need to find something else anyway.

What other choice did she have? Scan the classifieds for some crummy rental that fit in her budget?

She sighed. "I just need to stand on my own two feet."

She might get knocked down, but she wouldn't stay down.

"Agnes, your stubborn pride is your biggest flaw. You know that, right? I won't even be here. You'll have the house to yourself and can do plenty of standing."

Agnes glanced at the freshly tilled garden that ran along the property separating Mama's from Ian's parents'. "When are you planning to leave?"

"Well, now, that depends on you. If you agree, then I can fly out next week."

"Why so soon?"

"Why not? The sooner I get out there, the sooner I can help Memaw." Mama wrapped an arm around Agnes's shoulders and gave her a side hug. "This benefits both of us. You'll see."

No use in arguing with Mama once something stuck in her head.

Agnes's eyes drifted to Ian talking with Nick Brennan and Stephen Chase. What would he think of her being next door for the summer?

More important, would *she* even be able to think of living next door to him?

Maybe they could spend some time on the dock the way they did in the past. Maybe she could put her lingering feelings for him to rest once and forever.

Not likely.

Ian wandered over to the table for a piece of Mary's birthday cake. He wanted to see Red more than he wanted that cake.

All afternoon he tried to keep from staring at her, but

with the way the yellow sleeveless dress twirled around her shapely legs or her laugh floated through the air…it was a wonder he had managed to score any points playing cornhole.

Now that the others had decided to take a break, he snuck away before they started a new game.

"Nice party, Red." He shoved his hands in the front pockets of his Dockers and leaned against the deck railing.

"Thanks, Ian. I hear your team won."

"Yes, the red team scored twenty-one points first. Oh, yeah, we rock."

"Nice to see you're a gracious winner. Want some cake?"

"Sure. Thanks." He took the paper plate she held out to him and dug his fork through the white frosting and put it into his mouth. "It's good. So, how many pieces have you had?"

"That's not important. You just enjoy your cake."

"Manning the cake table? Pretty sweet setup, if you ask me. You can have your cake, and no one will notice if you have an extra piece or two…or six." He winked and shoved another bite in his mouth.

"I don't believe anyone asked. A gentleman wouldn't notice such things." Agnes pinched a glob of frosting off the corner of his piece and stuck it in her mouth.

"You okay?"

"Why do you ask?"

"I see the smile, but the light in your eyes is snuffed out."

"I'm wearing sunglasses, Ian. Little hard to see any kind of light. Mama invited me to spend the summer here while she hangs out with my memaw back in Texas."

Ian's stomach jumped. His eyes skimmed his parents' house that edged Mary's property.

Agnes next door all summer?

Yes, please.

In his head, he did a few fist pumps and shouted, *Woo-hoo!* at the top of his lungs. He shrugged. "That'd be cool."

"Maybe."

"Maybe? Why's that? You and your mom get along pretty well."

"Yes, we do, but she won't be here if I say yes."

"What's the problem? She doesn't want to go?"

"She does, and I'm sure she'll have a great time. It's just…"

"So what's holding you back?"

"I'm a little old to be moving home again."

"There's a difference between house-sitting and moving back in. I moved back home to help Mom and Dad with Griffin. It's definitely not permanent."

"True. If I'm not paying rent for the summer, then I could put that money toward a down payment for the cottage."

"So it sounds like a win-win for everyone." Including him.

With Red next door—even for a couple of months—he could show her he was more than a buddy, the guy next door, but the guy she needed to marry.

But right now he had to get something off his chest… something that wouldn't make her happy.

He jerked his head toward the lake. "Wanna go for a walk?"

Red waved a hand across the yard. "I can't leave the party."

"Just to the dock. I need to talk to you about something."

"What's going on? You look serious."

"Let's walk."

He waited while she crossed the yard to tell Mary where she was headed. Mary lifted a hand and waved. He returned the gesture, then smothered a smile as Mary and her friends put their heads together behind Red's back. He could only imagine what they were saying. And he figured Red wouldn't like it.

They cut through the shrubs that ran between both properties. Ian shoved his hands in his front pockets. It would've been so easy to slip his fingers around hers. But she'd probably slap him or shove him into the chilly lake.

The gravel path coiled through the trees. Red teetered on the stones in those ridiculous heels.

She stopped and placed a hand on his arm. "Hold on. I have a pebble in my shoe."

"Wear something practical, and you wouldn't have to worry about it."

"What do you know about fashion? You live in faded jeans, shorts or dress pants when you have to be in the office." Red slipped the sandal off her foot and brushed away the bits of gravel.

"Woman, one of these days you're going to break a leg wearing those crazy things."

"At least I'll look cute doing it."

"Believe me, Red, you could ditch the shoes and still outshine every female in this town." He caught a movement behind her.

A garter snake slithered across the path less than a foot behind her. If she looked back...

Grasping under her arms, he pulled her to her feet and wrapped her against his chest.

She pushed away and stared at him as if he'd lost his mind. "What's that all about?"

Ian tightened his arms and glanced over her shoulder. The weeds swayed as the snake disappeared. "I didn't want you to back up and sit on the garter snake behind you."

She screeched, causing him to wince and drop his ear to his shoulder, and practically jumped into his arms. Not that he was complaining. "Relax, Red. It's gone."

He turned her gently so she stood behind him but could see the clear path. He reached for her hand, giving it a little tug. "Come on. Let's go sit on the dock. I'll protect you."

"Thanks for not laughing at me, Ian." She clung to his arm and rested her head against his shoulder.

He lifted his arm and wrapped it around her, squeezing gently. If only he could hold her for the next fifty or sixty years. "I'll tease you about a lot of things, but your fears aren't one of them." He held her hand as she stepped over a muddy patch between the end of the path and the beginning of the dock.

Waves lapped at the shore. A frog croaked in the weeds. Somewhere along the water's edge, a couple of ducks quacked, joining in the chorus. Baked earth mingled with the fishy scent permeating the air.

Red's heels clomped on the wooden dock. Their shadows stretched over the blue water. Dad's old aluminum rowboat rocked and knocked against the dock. Tall grasses sprouted between the weathered boards.

At the end of the dock, they settled in two sun-warmed Adirondack chairs, one painted lemon-yellow and the other fire-engine red.

Agnes pushed her sunglasses on top of her head and raised her face toward trails of late afternoon sunshine streaking across the dusky sky. She didn't say anything for a moment. Sliding her glasses back on her face, she faced him. "So, what did you want to talk to me about?"

Sighing, Ian rested his head against the back of the chair, kicked off his shoes and toed off his dress socks. "I wish I didn't have to tell you this."

"What's the matter? Did you find someone who wasn't afraid of her own shadow in that place?"

"No, nothing like that." He scrubbed a hand over his face. "It's just that…well, there may not be an Agape House."

"Why? What happened?"

Ian pushed himself out of his chair and stood on the edge of the dock. He curled his toes over the rough-edged boards and crossed his arms over his chest to ease some of the pressure building behind his ribs.

"Dad's been against this project from the beginning, but Mom wants Zoe to have the best chance at a new life. When Dad learned Mom had signed the papers on behalf of the board, he packed a bag and headed for the cabin."

"He moved out?"

Ian shrugged. "He didn't come home last night."

"So that's why he didn't come today?" She stood and moved next to him, putting a hand on his shoulder. "I'm so sorry, Ian. What does Pete have against Agape House?"

"He had a rough childhood with alcoholic parents. He used to preach to us about the dangers of alcohol. After Zoe's arrest, Dad hasn't been the same. He resigned from the city council, stepped down from the church board and holes up in his office. He refuses to visit her in prison."

"But she's his daughter."

He rolled up his pant legs and dropped his feet in the water. He sucked in a breath at the shock of cold against his warm feet. "Try telling him that. He's acting like a jerk. Mom's upset. Griff keeps asking questions we can't answer."

"What does your mama want to do?"

"Keep her marriage together and bring her daughter home. Dad's demanding the impossible."

"Well, we need to talk some sense into him." Red slipped off her sandals and sat next to him, dipping her toes in the water.

"We?" He loved the way she teamed with him, but this was his family's problem. She had her own issues to work out.

"I have a stake in this now, too, you know." She bumped her shoulder against his.

Right, the cottage.

The sunlight dripped across the top of her head, catching the ginger glints in her hair and shading her face. She appeared to be sixteen instead of thirty-six.

His thoughts drifted back a couple of decades and remembered their almost daily talks on the docks. Seemed that no matter what the problem was, they could work it out sitting here with their feet in the water. If only things could be resolved as simply now.

He reached for her hand and laced his fingers through hers, squeezing gently. "This is not your problem, Red."

She lifted their joined hands and kissed his knuckles before releasing her fingers. "Your daddy will come around."

He loved the feel of her lips against his skin. He'd take the knuckle kiss for now, but one of these days he hoped for the chance to feel her lips on his. And not in the name of friendship either.

"How about if I pay Pete a visit and see if I can talk to him?"

He scowled at her. The woman didn't listen. "No, Red. You're not fighting my battles."

"Don't be a fool, Ian." She dipped her hand in the water and flicked his face. "Maybe Pete just needed to be reminded about the power of second chances."

Ian jerked as the icy drops landed on his hot skin. He wiped his eyes with the hem of his shirt. "How can restoring my family be pulling us apart?"

Agnes lifted her feet out of the water and stood. She brushed off the back of her dress, then reached for her sandals. "Like you said yesterday—sometimes it takes peeling away the layers to find the promise for the future."

Chapter Four

Agnes parked her restored 1964 Dodge Dart convertible in front of the James family cabin by the lake, shut off the engine and tossed her scarf onto the red vinyl passenger seat. She slid out from behind the wheel and slammed the door, the sound echoing along the hillside.

The afternoon wind stirred the pines, maples and oaks cradling the cabin. The upturned leaves and air saturated with humidity signaled rain close at hand.

She crossed the gravel parking area and faced the log cabin that had been in the James family for over one hundred years.

Decades of sunshine aged the hand-cut logs to a weathered gray. She climbed the three wide steps, passed the black rocker by the door and lifted the duck-shaped door knocker on the russet-stained pine door.

"It's open," a deep voice boomed from inside.

Agnes opened the door and sucked in a breath tinged with paint solvent and coffee. "Hey, Pete."

Pete James glanced over his shoulder, then turned back to the large canvas resting on a wooden easel standing in front of the window facing the lake. "Agnes Joy, to what do I owe the pleasure?"

Dressed in khaki shorts and a red T-shirt, he held a splattered palette in one hand and brandished crimson paint against the canvas like an expert swordsman. He wore a James & Son Insurance baseball hat backward on his head, covering his cropped salt-and-pepper hair.

Agnes crossed the hardwood floor and dropped a kiss on his whiskered cheek. "Ian's caught up with a client and asked if I'd swing by and pick up Griffin for him. They're leaving for Vanderfield in about forty-five minutes."

"Bubba's in the yard, playing fetch with Amos." He nodded toward the window where Griffin threw a yellow tennis ball overhand. The golden retriever leaped in the air and caught the ball in his strong jaws.

"Missed you at Mama's birthday yesterday."

"Give Mary my best." He offered no other explanation for his absence. Instead he continued to paint.

"What are you working on?"

"Cowboy in a canyon. Trying to steal as much natural light as I can before the cloud cover takes it away."

"It's quite muggy out there."

"Rain's in the forecast."

She didn't come to talk about the weather. Picking up Griffin was a decent excuse to try and get Pete to see some reason. Her nerves cinched the loose knot in her stomach.

"Pete, when we moved to Shelby Lake, you helped Daddy dry out, giving us a second chance at being a real family."

"Agnes Joy, I love your company, but if my family sent you to change my mind, you'd best grab Bubba and head on your way."

Just like Pete to speak his mind.

"Are you kidding? If Ian knew I was talking about this,

he'd be madder than a wet hen. I'm just saying without you, Daddy would've struggled to stay sober."

"Chuck was tougher than you think, Agnes." Pete set down his brush to reach for his coffee cup. "The choice was his."

"Agape House can be the second chance Zoe needs to turn her life around—like my daddy did." Agnes pressed her back against the windowsill, enjoying the warm air whispering across her neck. "How can you turn your back on your daughter?"

"Ever hear of tough love, Agnes?"

"There's tough love, and there's rejection."

She spied a stack of canvases leaning below the window. Without asking for permission, she flipped through them, stopping at the last one that showed two sets of hands—larger ones cupping a smaller set that held a butterfly. Recognizing the wing-shaped birthmark on the smaller hand, Agnes realized Pete had painted Zoe's hands.

Oh, Pete...

Staring at the canvas, Pete wiped his hands on a rag, then walked to the window. With his back to her, he stared out at the trees and the lake.

"When I was a little older than Bubba, my parents died on Christmas Eve because they were too drunk to drive and decided to walk home. Instead they passed out in a snowbank and froze to death. No matter how many times they promised to change, they didn't. Made me realize words were meaningless without actions to back them up."

"Oh, Pete, I can't even imagine." Tears filled Agnes's eyes. "You were a kid—you couldn't have changed your parents. But you can help others get their lives back on track now."

Pete whirled around, his eyebrows raised and his lips thinned. "People don't change, Agnes. They tell you what you want to hear. Then the minute temptation strikes, they're back to screwing up their lives again. Char and Ian will pour themselves into that place only to end disappointed when those women fall back into their old habits."

"Give your family this chance to prove Zoe can turn her life around."

"And when she doesn't? What then? She'll end up back behind bars, but she will have destroyed my wife, my son, my grandson...I can't take that chance. I need to protect them."

"How much protecting are you doing by holing up here instead of trying to work things out with your wife?"

A muscle jumped in the side of Pete's jaw. He looked at her. "When did you get so sassy?"

"I've always been sassy, Pete. Much to my mama's shame. You're scared...nothing wrong with admitting it. Just don't let that fear keep you from missing out on the incredible blessings God has in store for your family. I promise you—that's one regret you will be responsible for."

Amos barked from the porch a second before Griffin flung open the screen door and crashed into the room. "Agnes, what are you doing here?"

She blinked rapidly to dismiss the evidence of her emotions and stretched a Texas-sized smile across her face. With purposeful strides, she crossed the room and flung an arm around his sweaty shoulders. "I came to pick up the cutest boy in the county and take him back to his uncle."

"Let me know when you find him." The kid smirked as he headed for the sink. He filled up a glass with water, drank half, then poured the rest in Amos's dish next to the stove.

His dark hair plastered to his sweaty head. Dirt skimmed his legs below the hem of his red basketball shorts. His yellow Shelby Lake Lions Soccer T-shirt had a tear in the hem. Not the best duds to wear to see his mama. Maybe he had time for a quick shower.

As if reading her mind, Pete nodded toward the staircase. "Hey, Bubba, grab a quick shower and put on clean clothes, but make it snappy because Agnes needs to get you back."

"Okay, Grandpa. I bet I can be back down in five minutes, Agnes."

"Take time to wash."

"Yeah, yeah."

He scampered up the steps with Amos on his trail.

Before Agnes could resume her conversation with Pete, tires crunched in the driveway. A minute later, footsteps thumped on the porch; then Ian filled the doorway, a frown creasing his forehead. "What gives, Red? I thought you were meeting me to drop off Griffin."

She glanced at her watch and swallowed a groan, then nodded toward Pete, who had his back to them. "I was talking with Pete and lost track of time."

Ian's eyes narrowed and a muscle jumped in the side of his jaw. He dropped his voice to a whisper. "About what?"

"The weather…rain is in the forecast."

"Where's Bubba? We need to get going." He didn't acknowledge his dad.

How could those two be in the same room and not say as much as a "hello"?

Agnes sighed and her eyes darted toward the staircase. "He's in the shower but promises to be down in five."

"Fine. I'll wait outside." Ian turned and pushed through the door.

"Ian…" She tossed a glance at Pete, who exhaled loudly and removed his ball cap to rake his hands through his hair. Feeling torn, she ventured onto the porch to check on Ian.

She found him around the corner, leaning on the railing. She touched his shoulder. "You okay?"

"Fine." The flared nostrils and thinned lips betrayed his words.

"I didn't mean to lose track of time."

"Don't sweat it. I can make up the time on the road." He stared at the lake but clenched his jaw. "Did you and Dad have a nice little chat…about the weather?"

She refused to let his sarcastic tone ruffle her feathers. She crossed her arms and pressed her back against the railing. "Did I fight your battles? No. Did I stir the hornet's nest? Maybe. We're in this together, Ian. So stop your sulking, because you asked me to be a part of this."

She longed to ease the worry and frustration from his brow. Pete and Ian shared many traits, including their stubbornness. She just hoped they'd come to a compromise before their family fell apart.

Little boys should be spending Saturday mornings eating sugary cereal while sprawled in front of the TV or kicking a soccer ball across the field. Not riding three hours to visit their mother in prison.

Griffin stared out the backseat window. Ian could only imagine what he'd thought of this trip every other Saturday for the past four years.

At least they didn't have to make the trek alone.

He glanced at Red sitting in the passenger seat. "Sorry for being a jerk earlier. Thanks again for coming with us."

"You've thanked me three times now. I get it—you're appreciative…or else a big chicken to come by yourself." She smiled to show she was teasing.

No, that wasn't it…he simply wanted to spend as much time with her as he could.

And he did feel badly for acting like a jerk at the cabin. But that wasn't her fault. Dad wouldn't even look him in the eye like a man and say hello. But then he didn't make much of an effort to greet him either. So they were both to blame.

Ian tightened his grip on the steering wheel as he approached the front gate of Vanderfield Women's State Correctional Institution. He shifted the engine into Park and reached for his wallet. "I need your driver's license."

"I know the drill. Not my first rodeo." She reached for her purse, dug the card out of her wallet and handed it to him.

He took it, then snagged Griffin's state ID card out of the cup holder and handed all three IDs to the stern gray-uniformed guard.

Without a smile, the man checked their names against his visitors' clipboard. He handed them back to Ian, then buzzed the front gate. "Have a nice day."

"You, too."

The gates slid back, allowing Ian to drive down the familiar lane to the visitors' parking lot in front of the prison that looked more like an old college than a correctional facility. Except for the snipers in the watchtowers and the rolled razor wire atop the high electric fencing surrounding the compound.

As soon as Ian shut off the engine, Griffin unbuckled his seat belt and scampered out the back door. Red rounded the front of the SUV and joined them. She ruffled Griffin's hair. "Ready to go?"

"Yes. Did I tell you Mom's training a new dog?" Griffin shielded his eyes as he looked at Red and shared about his mother's participation in the prison's canine training program.

"No, you didn't. What kind?"

"A yellow Lab named Otis. She's had him for two weeks. He sleeps with her and everything."

"That's cool. How long will she train this one?"

"She said eight weeks altogether."

"Have you seen him yet?" Red finger-combed Griffin's hair away from his face and straightened the collar on his red polo shirt.

"Nah, but Mom described him in her letter."

"Let's get inside so you can see him." Placing a hand at the base of Griffin's neck, Ian guided him toward the visitors' entrance.

Inside the door, they emptied their pockets. Ian dropped his wallet, phone and car keys in a bin. Agnes placed her purse in another bin. They allowed Ian to keep three dollars in change to buy snacks while visiting Zoe.

Griffin ran ahead and pulled on the heavy glass door that opened into the visitors' area.

Cinder block walls painted tan, green vinyl-covered chairs and several scarred wooden tables filled the room. Inmates and their families sat at most of the tables. Griffin scuttled to their usual place in the corner closest to the snack machine and pulled out a chair, its feet screeching against the gleaming tile floor.

Ian gave their names to the guard standing watch near the entrance to the prison cell blocks. He placed his hand on the small of Red's back and guided her toward the table where Griffin sat on the edge of his chair, bouncing his knee and keeping his eyes glued to the door leading to the cells.

The kid's excitement at seeing his mom made Ian more determined than ever to get Agape House up and running.

About five minutes later, a door buzzed.

Zoe entered the room with Otis, the new yellow Lab Griffin mentioned his mom training as part of her role in the prison's dog training program for almost three years.

"Mom!" A grin crossed Griffin's face. He bolted out of his chair, but Ian caught him around the waist and pulled him back.

"You have to stay at the table. Remember? We can't break the rules."

"Sorry. I just want to give her a hug." His bottom lip popped out.

Red draped an arm around his shoulders. "As soon as she comes to the table, you can."

With her dark hair pulled back into a ponytail and wearing the issued prison orange and tan slip-on shoes, Zoe hurried to their table and commanded Otis to sit.

Griffin pushed off Red's arm and flung himself at his mother. Zoe crushed him against her chest and buried her face into his neck. She brushed his hair off his forehead and kissed his temple, tears glazing her eyes.

Ian blinked back the wetness that warmed the backs of his eyes and swallowed the lump clogging his throat.

Their greetings and departures got to him every time.

Red reached for his hand and squeezed gently. He returned the gesture, thankful for the hundredth time she had agreed to join them today. He hated these trips, but he'd do it for Griffin and Zoe.

Ian caught the scowl marring the guard's face. They discouraged prolonged physical contact. What damage could a kid hugging his mother do? But they needed to play by the rules so they could keep visiting.

He caught her in a hug, then disengaged Griffin's arms

from around his mother's neck. "Come on, Bubba. Let your mom sit."

After giving Red a quick hug, Zoe sat on one side and they sat across from her, as was procedure. A hug at greeting and one at departure, but no physical contact during the visit.

Ian didn't need to look under the table to know Zoe had her hands balled into fists in her lap. Her eyes drank in Griffin's appearance, longing creasing her face. Longing that made him even more determined to bring his sister home. While Griffin filled his mom in on what was happening at school and with soccer, Ian waited for a pause in their conversation to bring up the latest with Agape House.

"And Grandma bought a house. Grandpa's been staying at the cabin."

Zoe jerked her gaze to Ian. "Why did Mom buy a house? And what's going on with Dad?"

Ian stretched out a leg and shoved his hand in his front pocket. He pulled out a handful of change. "Griff, I think your mom looks a little thirsty, don't you? How about going to the pop machine and getting her a Dr Pepper?"

"Sure. Is that what you want, Mom?"

"A Dr Pepper would be great. But only if you have one, too."

"You want one, Agnes?"

"Sure, I could use a Coke. How about if I come with you to help carry the cans?" Red started to stand, but Griffin waved for her to sit.

"I can handle it."

She smiled. "I'm sure you can."

"What about you, Uncle Ian?"

"No, thanks, Bubba." Ian dropped the change into Griffin's hand.

Griffin slid back his chair and headed for the pop machine against the cinder block wall.

Ian turned back to Zoe. "The board finally found a place for Agape House. Mom signed the papers last weekend. Agnes will be heading the volunteer committee to clean up and repaint the inside. I'm going to do the work on the roof and the other outside stuff. Mom's pushing to have it ready before your hearing in August."

"So, why is Dad staying at the cabin?"

Ian sighed and rubbed his thumb and forefinger over his eyes. "He's having a hard time dealing with all of this." He really didn't want to go into details. Not here. Especially with Griffin there, too.

Zoe didn't respond to Ian's last comment. She dropped her eyes to the table and traced a gouge with her thumbnail. "It's a great program, Ian. And I truly appreciate what you're all doing...."

"But?"

"But you can't do this for me." She met his gaze and slumped against her chair.

He hated the defeat weighing her down. "What? Of course we can. You're my sister."

"I'm also a grown woman who needs to make her own choices and do what's best for me. Stop trying to protect me."

Why did they have this same conversation every time he visited? Ian struggled to school his tone. "How about what's best for Griffin? He needs his mother. Think of the other women who will benefit from this, too. And those kids who will have their moms back in their lives."

"You and Mom and Dad are doing a great job with him. So much more than I ever could. Even when I'm out, he'll be better off with you guys."

Ian ground his teeth together. Forcing himself to relax,

he glanced at Griffin feeding coins into the soda machine. "Would you like to put that to a vote? Because I guarantee you'll lose. The kid's counting down the days, sis. Each night he prays for you and crosses out another day on the calendar hanging on his wall. Tell me that's a kid who's better off without his mom. Stop thinking about yourself and focus on him."

She glared at him and blinked back tears. "Every waking minute is filled with thoughts of him, so don't lecture me."

Red reached across the table and touched Zoe's balled fist, but Ian pulled it back and gave her a slight shake of his head. He leaned close to her ear. "No physical contact allowed."

"I forgot." Pink stole across Red's cheeks. She gave Zoe an apologetic smile. "I'm sorry, Zoe."

"It is what it is." Zoe sighed and smoothed a hand over her hair. "What kind of life do you think he'll have when I'm out? My choices will affect him for the rest of his life. When he gets married and has kids. And those kids ask about his daddy. What's he going to say then? Oh, my mom killed him in an accident because she drove drunk. He's better off without me—you all are. Who wants a criminal for a mother?"

Ian had no answers. He rested an elbow on the table and cupped a hand around his jaw.

Red's eyes darted between Ian and Zoe. She kept her voice neutral as she spoke, "Zoe, you're right...to a point."

Ian jerked a look at her. What was she up to?

She held up a hand, gesturing for him to chill out. She directed her gaze at Zoe. "Your choices have affected Griffin's life, and they will since you're his parent. But he's not better off without you. He loves you and sees a mom, not a criminal. Now's your chance to be the kind of mom he deserves. That's a choice only you can make."

"But what if I can't do it. What if I screw up again?"

Ian reached for Zoe's hand, then pulled back, remembering the no physical contact rule. "Zoe, you don't have to go it alone. We're here to help. After all, that's what family is all about."

Chapter Five

Would she ever get to a point when she didn't want to run in the other direction when this house came into view?

At least this time she didn't freak out just stepping through the door.

Agnes drew in a lungful of fresh air as she followed Charlotte James inside. A glance over her shoulder showed Ian standing on the threshold. Was he trying to ward off an escape attempt?

Her flip-flops slapped against the entryway floor. She set her bucket of cleaning supplies next to the door, then dug in her tote bag for a notebook, pen, metal tape measure and camera.

Her cutoffs and yellow tank top made her feel grungy next to Charlotte's white blouse, navy trousers, pearl earrings and silver hair caught neatly in a clip.

Charlotte turned and placed a hand on Agnes's arm. "You sure about this, honey?"

Agnes glanced at her friend's long narrow polished fingers, veins mapping the backs of her soft hands.

The past week had turned her life upside down. But

she refused to let the bad memories in this house win. She'd fight back. Especially after their visit with Zoe.

Griffin needed his mama back home where she belonged. Agnes would do whatever she needed to help make that happen.

She pasted on a smile and wrapped an arm around Charlotte's shoulders. "I gave you my word, and I'm not going to let you down."

The scrunched lines on Charlotte's forehead softened. "You let me know if it gets to be too much."

"I'll be fine. Let's get started." Agnes led them into the living room, then stopped. "The ugly carpet is gone."

Charlotte's heels clicked against the exposed wooden floor. "I asked a couple of guys from church to rip it out yesterday."

"Good." Agnes marched to the window and shoved it open, taking a moment to breathe in the afternoon breeze. She turned away from the window to find Charlotte checking out the living room while Ian leaned against the doorframe checking out…her.

Her skin warmed under his gaze. She tugged on the hem of her tank top, trying not to let his watchful eyes unnerve her.

What was he thinking? Waiting for her to crack and run like last time?

She walked over to Charlotte, but the back of her neck prickled. She didn't have to look over her shoulder to know Ian's eyes followed her.

What was his problem?

Charlotte trailed her fingers along the mantel, then brushed the dust from her hands. "We have a lot of work to do to get this place ready."

"Mom, we'll have it done in time. Stop worrying." Ian's deep voice echoed off the bare walls as he moved away from the doorjamb and placed his hands on Charlotte's shoulders. "Red and her merry band of volunteers won't let you down."

"Not worrying…I know everything will work out." She reached for Agnes's notebook and clicked the pen. "I'll write while you take pictures or do whatever you need. What do you envision for this room?"

Hands on hips, Agnes walked a slow circle around the room, trying not to let the despair weigh her down. "Hmm, what do you think about soft green walls, cream-colored draperies and perhaps an area rug with shades of green and tan? Doeskin-colored furniture, patterned throw pillows and chairs upholstered in the same print would complement the room. And maybe lamps on small tables for warm lighting."

"I like that." Charlotte jotted notes, then glanced at Ian, who squatted and ran his hand over a buckled section in the floor. "What are you looking at, Ian?"

"These floors will need to be sanded. Otherwise we may have a tripping hazard with these uneven boards. We can't risk a lawsuit by having someone get hurt."

"I'll add that to the to-do list. What do you think of Agnes's suggestions?"

Ian rubbed a hand across his jaw. "Maybe we should keep the walls white."

Agnes scrunched up her face. "White? These women have been looking at prison drab for who knows how long? Let's give them something to refresh their spirits."

He looked up with eyebrows raised. "You think they'll care?"

Did he know *anything* about women?

"Absolutely. We want this home to be welcoming from the moment they walk through the door."

"That's the first time you called this house a home."

Ian straightened and dusted the dirt off the seat of his jeans.

Agnes shrugged. "It will be by the time I'm finished with it."

"Ernie at Shelby Lake Hardware offered three five-gallon buckets of white paint. If you want each room a different color, that's almost twenty-five bucks a can. That'll eat at our budget. Then we won't have a house in any color, no matter how welcoming you want it to be."

"You've got to trust my judgment, Ian. I can stay within budget, no matter the wall color."

"I do trust you, Red, but why is wall color a big deal?"

"It determines the rest of the decisions about furnishings."

What was it about men and this house, thinking they had to make all the decisions? She and Bobby had had a similar argument when they moved in. Of course, he won. "Like I said—trust my judgment or find someone else to oversee this."

"Mom, what do you think?"

"Oh, sure. Go to your mama." Agnes threw her hands in the air and rolled her eyes. "Of course she's going to side with you."

Charlotte looked up from her notes and crossed her arms. "I haven't heard you two bicker like this since that Shelby Lake Golden Paddle race you did together and nearly flipped your canoe."

Ian jerked a thumb over his shoulder at Agnes. "If she would have sat like I told her, then we wouldn't have tipped."

Agnes planted her hands on her hips. "If you hadn't been showing off for Nikki Pearson, then the boat wouldn't have been rocking."

Charlotte dropped the notepad on the mantel and

raised her hands. "Doesn't matter who was right and who was wrong. You took first place and made it home before the storm hit. Now let's talk about something we can change." She turned to Ian. "You two make a great team because eventually you do manage to compromise. Agnes is right—these rooms do need personality."

Agnes wrangled her tongue to keep it from slipping between her lips in a childish gesture.

Then Charlotte turned to her. "Agnes, Ian's right about the budget—we don't have a lot of wiggle room. When community business owners are willing to donate, we use what they're offering. They receive free advertising in exchange for their generosity."

Agnes peeked at Ian over Charlotte's shoulder and rolled her eyes at his silent *na-na-na* taunt.

"Let's stick to white walls, but allow Agnes to choose the accent colors of each room. We do need to trust her judgment, Ian. She's not going to tell you how to fix the roof."

"Give her time." Ian's grumble made Agnes's lips twitch, but she kept quiet. No sense in poking the bear.

Charlotte's cell phone chimed. She retrieved it from the side pocket of her purse and glanced at the screen. "I have to take this. Think you two can handle the rest of the house without adult supervision?"

"I'm ready to start scrubbing. Some of my best ideas come while elbow deep in Lysol water."

"No problem. At least allow Ian to give you a tour of the upstairs so you have an idea of what we're working with to help with your brainstorming."

"No need, Charlotte. I used to live here, remember? I know the upstairs better than both of you." She gestured across the ceiling. "Bedroom. Bedroom. Full bath. Bedroom. And down the little hall, another small bedroom."

The same room she planned to paint yellow and decorate with zoo animals.

"Oh, that's right." She gave them quick hugs, then headed to the front door.

Ian glanced at his watch. "Griffin's going to be home from school soon. I need to meet his bus. Then we'll come back and give you a hand."

"Don't worry about me. Do your thing. I'm going to start scrubbing these walls to get them ready to paint." Agnes headed for the entryway to retrieve the bucket of cleaning supplies.

Ian reached for her elbow as she brushed past. "Try to understand, Red."

Agnes glanced at his face, then looked away, shrugging. "I feel like you're trying to control what I do."

"I have to answer to the board about how much we spend. I don't want to waste it on something as trivial as paint."

"This isn't about paint, but you not letting me do the job you hired—" Agnes made air quotes around the word *hired* "—me to do. If you want to micromanage every detail, then find someone else to coordinate, because I'm not going to be controlled in this house again."

"I'm not Bobby, Red." He glanced at his watch again. "Even though you're familiar with the upstairs, I'm not. Let's check it out quickly before I have to get Griffin."

Her eyes jerked to the staircase, a coil of unease twisting in the pit of her stomach. Had he forgotten the meltdown from the other day? "You go ahead."

"Red, I understand your hesitation, but put your painful past to rest. I'll help you—one step at a time." He stretched out a hand toward her.

Ian was right—she couldn't let the staircase haunt her

forever. And with him being there, maybe it wouldn't be as daunting.

Agnes trudged to the staircase, placed one hand on the nicked banister and put her other in his. His fingers enveloped hers, radiating strength and warmth. She gave him a wobbly smile.

He nodded toward the stairs and tugging gently on her arm. Her chest tightened.

"Take one step, Red."

As she placed a foot on the next step, hazy images from the past rose before her eyes like mist floating over the lake. She squeezed her eyes shut to prevent them from coming into focus.

Her heart thrummed as she forced air into her lungs and took another step. Sweat beaded on her upper lip. She lifted a shaky hand to wipe it away. Her stomach churned.

"You're doing great." Ian's tone reminded her of listening to Nick coaxing Noah into taking his first steps.

Heat curled up her neck and settled across her cheeks. She didn't need to be encouraged like a toddler. She was a grown woman. She could do this.

She let go of Ian's hand and took a couple more steps.

Ian went ahead a few steps and turned, his wide shoulders blocking her view up the stairs. He scowled, then swept an open palm above her head.

She flinched. For only a split second.

"Red?"

She hadn't realized she had closed her eyes until she opened them to find him standing in front of her. She put her hands up and stepped back but lost her footing.

He reached out and caught her.

Her heart picked up speed as she became aware of his tight grip on her arms. The way he stood over her with that scowl...she disappointed him, too. Would he think she wasn't worthy of being a part of this project? Or would he tire of her and find someone else? Someone who wouldn't challenge his suggestions?

Ian's eyes widened. He released her gently and took a step back with hands raised.

What had she done?

She blinked several times until clarity erased the fog around her brain. Then reality set in.

She turned and hurried down the couple of steps, not wanting to see the pity in his eyes, and drew in a shuddering breath.

"Red?"

In through the nose, out through the mouth.

The focused breathing slowed her racing heart.

"There was a spiderweb hanging down. I didn't want you to run into it." He touched her elbow gently, his voice quiet, almost whisperlike. "I would never hurt you."

"I know, Ian." Her voice sounded raspy.

She dropped her gaze to the thirsty, neglected floor.

She needed to bring lemon oil. To rub it into the wood. To bring back the shine.

Ian moved in front of her, lifted her chin with his index finger and scanned her face. A muscle jumped in the side of his jaw as he clenched his teeth. "Why…" Ian stepped away and dragged a hand threw his hair. "Why didn't you tell me?" His voice caught on the last word.

She bit her bottom lip to steady her trembling jaw and blinked away pressure building behind her eyes. A tear slipped over her lower lashes and trailed down her cheek.

"It was only a couple of times." Her shame had surfaced, and now what would he think of her?

"Once is too many. You hear me?" Ian crushed her to his chest. "Why didn't you come to me? I would have protected you."

The anguish in his gentle tone severed her last band of restraint. She twisted her fists into the folds of his T-shirt and soaked the fabric with her tears. His arms curled around her, his cheek resting on the top of her head.

Her chest shuddered as her tears dried on her cheeks. She rubbed the back of her hand over her eyes, trying to erase the evidence of her humiliation.

She should move away. She should apologize. She should make notes about the other rooms. She should race up the stairs to prove she wasn't a coward.

But, for that moment, she just wanted to rest her ear against his chest and listen to his beating heart.

The fibers of his T-shirt held the scent of his laundry detergent mixed with his deodorant. The strength of his embrace shielded her from her haunted past, melting her fears.

Ian pulled back and cradled her face with both hands, his fingers threading in her hair. He kept his gaze steady with hers. "No one will ever hurt you again. Ever. You are safe with me."

As his words soaked in, Agnes searched his face and cupped his jaw. "I know."

She placed a hand on his chest, feeling his rapid heartbeat beneath her palm. Filled with a courage she lacked moments ago, Agnes rose on her tiptoes and brushed a gentle kiss across his parted lips.

He disentangled his hands from her hair and placed them on her shoulders. His questioning eyes searched her face. "Red—"

She pressed a finger against his lips. "You're my dragon slayer, Ian. I feel safe here because of you."

Red had kissed him. And he should have been thrilled. But she was caught up in a whirlpool of emotions, and the kiss was meant as a thank-you. He couldn't read more into it.

The gentle brush of her lips over his…he wanted to drown himself in her embrace, but he'd done enough to spook her.

Still, he couldn't help remember the first kiss they'd shared all those years ago.

It was the night of her senior prom. After finishing finals, he'd come home for the summer a day early and escorted her to the dance after her date had come down with strep throat.

After the prom, they'd sat on the dock talking about their futures. She'd looked so beautiful in the moonlight that he'd seized the moment. Then she'd admitted she liked him more than a friend. And he'd turned her down.

What a fool he'd been. But he was only a sophomore in college, and she was about to head off to Texas for school. He hadn't wanted to tie her down.

Talk about wasted years, especially her time with Bobby.

If he had exposed his heart that night, then Red never would have had to suffer at that jerk's hands.

He swung the ax with both hands and split the log in two. Sweat soaked the bandanna tied around his forehead. His muscles trembled from exhaustion. He grabbed both pieces with gloved hands and stacked them on the growing pile behind the garage.

He arched his back, stretching out his muscles. His wet T-shirt stuck to his skin.

Thirty feet away, the lake lapped at the shore with a peaceful rhythm. Birds whistled and chirped from the trees overhead. Somewhere along the bank, a duck quacked. Sunshine danced on the surface of the water.

He breathed in the scent of pine, wet leaves and fresh air. A haven of rest and relaxation.

But he felt anything but refreshed.

He kicked up another short log with the toe of his beat-up work boot and steadied it on the tree stump. He brought the ax down with force. The split halves fell to the ground.

Kicking them out of the way, he picked up another piece of wood.

He'd continue splitting until he could erase what had happened before the kiss. He hadn't given a second thought to brushing away the spider. But now the fear in Red's eyes had been engraved in his memory.

He knew things hadn't been great with Red and Bobby for years before their marriage fell apart. At Bobby's request, well, more like demand, Ian kept his distance while they were married. But if she had even hinted Bobby hurt her, Ian would have made sure she didn't live with that fear again.

At least now he knew a little more why being in that house haunted her so much.

He didn't care if the man hit her only once. It was one time too many.

Mom rounded the corner of the garage. She'd changed out of her work clothes into jeans and a Shelby Lake Lions T-shirt. She handed him a glass of lemonade. "I thought you were going to have someone else cut up this dead tree and haul it away since you didn't have time.

"Change of plans." He took the glass and chugged half in a couple of gulps. He wiped his mouth with the back of his hand, then set the glass on the ground out of the way.

Mom surveyed the stack of wood behind the garage, then looked at him with concern. "Where's Griffin?"

"Jimmy invited him over for dinner." Ian nodded to

their neighbor's house, steadied another log on the stump and swung the ax.

"You okay?" Mom kneeled in front of the side flower bed that ran the length of the house and started weeding.

"He hit her, Mom." An ache swelled within the cavity of his chest, threatening to squeeze the breath from his lungs.

Mom looked up and twisted to sit on the rock border. "Who, honey?"

Ian whipped his soaked bandanna off and wiped his forehead with the sleeve of his grimy T-shirt. He swallowed several times. "That…jerk. Bobby. He hit her. And Red never told me."

"Oh, honey, how awful for her. I'm surprised Mary never said anything."

He brushed matted wood fibers off his sweaty arms. "She may not know."

Mom frowned. "Even though Agnes is a private person, I'd be surprised if she kept her mother in the dark about something like that. How did you find out?"

Ian relayed what had happened on the stairs at Agape House.

"Then what happened?"

"We…talked for a few minutes, and then I had to leave and get Griffin."

He hadn't wanted to leave her there alone to wrestle the ghosts by herself. He'd wanted to pull her into his arms and kiss her again. But he needed to take his time and wait until he could do it when she wouldn't mistake his intentions in any way.

"I think there's more. You know? Something else that happened that she's not telling me." He shared about Agnes bailing on him the first time they checked out the place together.

"You're a great friend, Ian. Being in that house is causing her to relive a painful time in her life. Be patient and willing to listen when she's ready to talk."

He reached for his glass and drained the rest of the lemonade. "I'm always here for her."

The sun dipped behind the trees as the evening breeze stirred the leaves with its cooling breath.

Ian walked to the edge of bank, slipped his hands in his back pockets and stared at the water. Mom followed, sticks crunching beneath her feet.

"What if she doesn't talk about it? What if she keeps it bottled up and has a meltdown, but I'm not there to protect her?"

"Honey, you can't be everyone's protector."

"I can be hers." His eyes burned from a mixture of sweat, wood dust and regret. "Why'd she have to marry that jerk?"

Mom laid a hand against his cheek. "Instead of you, you mean?"

"She should have been my wife." An ache swelled in his chest to the point where taking a breath was painful. "After she graduated, I wanted to marry her."

"Honey, you were both so young."

"Really? How old were you and Dad when you got married?"

"That was a different generation. Besides, you were in college and Agnes planned to attend school in Texas."

"When I told Dad I wanted to marry Red, he suggested I give her a little space to experience life before settling down. Then if I still wanted to marry her once she graduated, go for it. But I never got the chance. She ran to Bobby Levine…and look how that turned out."

"This is not your fault, Ian."

"She came to me after Bobby proposed and asked if

I knew of any reason why she and Bobby shouldn't get married."

"What did you tell her?"

"She needed to follow her heart. If Bobby was the man she wanted to marry, she needed to say yes. I told her no matter what she'd always be my best friend."

"What did you want her to say?"

"I wanted her to say she was making a mistake, call off the wedding and choose me. Instead she wasted ten years with a man who didn't deserve her."

"Now it's your chance to show her the man she deserves to spend the rest of her life with."

"She sees me as her best friend."

"Best friends make the best spouses. Change her heart, Ian. Otherwise you'll spend a lifetime regretting your decision."

Chapter Six

How did she accumulate so much stuff? And how was she going to fit it all in Mama's garage?

Agnes stood in the middle of her living room with boxes at her feet and a stack of newspapers on the ottoman. She picked up a pottery bowl and wrapped it in several layers of the *Shelby Lake Gazette* before tucking it in the box on the coffee table. Yesterday's news became today's packing material.

Sometimes she wished she could wrap her heart in paper to protect its fragile state.

Her cheeks burned as she thought about yesterday's panic attack. And that kiss. What had gotten into her?

Of course Ian wasn't going to hurt her.

If he started treating her like a breakable piece of pottery...well, she'd put a stop to that in a hurry. She might have a few nicks and scars, but she was fully functional.

The scent of newspaper mingled with the coffee brewing in the kitchen. She needed a break.

Placing her hands on the small of her back, she leaned backward to stretch her tired muscles.

A tap sounded on her screen door before it opened, and Ian poked his head inside. "Want a hand?"

Agnes straightened and finger-combed her hair into some semblance of order. "Sure, come on in. Feel free to move boxes or piles if you want a place to sit."

Ian shoved his hands in his front pockets on his olive cargo shorts. "Nah, I'm good. I stopped at Cuppa Josie's to see if you wanted to grab a bite to eat and catch a movie after work, but Josie said you left early."

"Like I had a choice. She practically booted me out the door. Want some iced tea? Or coffee?"

"Sweetened or unsweetened?" The corner of his mouth lifted.

Agnes shook her head. "You Yankees don't know how to drink your tea. I have both."

"I like keeping my teeth cavity free."

"I just made a fresh pot of coffee."

"Coffee's good. You should have texted or something. I would have given you a hand sooner."

Agnes headed for the kitchen and filled two stoneware mugs with coffee. "I appreciate that, but your hands are full already."

Ian followed her and leaned against the sink. "You sure that's all?"

"Of course. Why?" She pulled the hazelnut creamer out of the fridge and added a splash to each of their mugs.

"Well, after yesterday…"

Hands fisted on her hips, she turned to him. "Let's clear the air so you're not pussyfooting around me. I over-reacted yesterday. You'd never lay a hand on me, Ian. You're the kindest, gentlest person I know. That house seems to bring out my inner crazy."

He didn't say anything for a minute. The only sound in the kitchen was the clock above the sink and Ian's spoon clicking against his mug as he stirred his coffee. He set the spoon in the sink, then gave her a direct look. "You're not crazy, Red. I'm sorry for what you went through."

"It's in the past." She waved away his sympathy and reached for her cup, needing something to do with her hands. "Nothing for you to worry about."

"Apparently it is if you still react that way."

"I'm fine. It won't happen again. Can we talk about something else please?"

Ian looked as though he doubted her, but he didn't press it. "Why didn't you tell me?" Pain…and maybe frustration laced his quiet tones.

She stared at the coffee in her cup, not wanting to see the misery in his gaze. "Because."

He snorted. "Good answer."

"It was my problem, okay?" She set her cup on the small dinette table with more force than necessary. Coffee splashed over the rim. She snatched the dishcloth out of the sink and wiped up, hoping he didn't notice her trembling fingers.

"But I'm your friend." He cupped her face.

She stared into his blue eyes rimmed with black and canopied with arched eyebrows. His nostrils flared as his lips thinned. Unlike yesterday, this scowl didn't send her into a downward spiral.

She pulled his hands away from her face but didn't release his fingers. "Yes, you are. But your family was going through that mess with Zoe. If I had told you, then Pete and Charlotte would have had two children behind bars because you would have ripped Bobby apart."

Ian's eyes scanned her face as he processed her words. His frown softened. He stepped back and scrubbed a hand over his face. "You said your marriage was over because of Bobby's cheating."

Needing a little breathing room, she walked into the living room and picked up more paper to start wrapping the pictures lining her mantel. "And I didn't lie. That last woman was the final straw. I spent a month in Sweeney Hollow with Memaw, then returned to Shelby Lake to put the pieces of my broken heart back together. I never intended to step foot in that house again."

"Until I asked for your help. You should have told me why. We could have worked around it somehow."

"We Kingsleys keep our dirty laundry in the hamper where it belongs. Dealing with the rumors about Bobby's online gambling and other women were bad enough. I wasn't going to give anyone any more reasons to gossip about me."

"I'm not other people." Ian reached for a section of the paper and wrapped it around one of the photos.

"By the time I came back from Texas, I didn't want to rehash it anymore."

Ian surveyed the room cluttered with boxes. "When do you plan to be out of here?"

"By Friday. Mama decided to wait a week before flying out, so I'm taking her to the airport on Monday. That gives us the weekend to go over things with the house and the gardens."

She reached for the last frame—her favorite, actually—of the two of them when they were kids lying on the dock, rocking late '80s acid-washed shorts and neon shirts. She handed it to him to wrap. "Nice mullet."

He grinned, his eyes crinkling at the corners. "That's quite a side ponytail you're sporting with the hot pink scrunchie. How old were we in this picture?"

"Twelve and fourteen. You told me you were going to youth camp for two weeks."

"Oh, that's right. And you missed me every minute I was gone."

"In your dreams, bub. More like you missed me."

Mama had taken their picture, then given it to Agnes the day Ian had left for camp. After his parents' station wagon had disappeared down the street, she had thundered up the steps to her room, slammed the door and sprawled across her bed, soaking her pillow with her tears. She spent the first week with her nose buried in her Judy Blume books. "That was the summer you broke your ankle playing kickball."

Completely convinced Ian would find a new friend and forget about her, she had prayed and asked God to bring him home early. Then spent the rest of the summer feeling guilty when he came home on crutches.

"And you refused to sign my cast. You made me a card instead." Ian set the wrapped frame in the box and taped the box closed. He uncapped a black marker with his teeth and scrawled *Fragile* across the top.

"I didn't want to be like everyone else."

"You're definitely an original, Red."

She wasn't sure what to make of that.

Ian's head ached as he tried to focus on Griffin's chatter about keeping from falling into the lava as he played Minecraft on Ian's iPad.

He pulled into the driveway at Agape House and cut the engine. Griffin looked up from his game. "What are we doing here?"

"Stopping to see if Red wants to join us for dinner. You mind?"

"Nope." Griffin dropped the tablet in his lap and looked out the windshield at the house. "You really think they'll let Mom come home?"

"Why do you ask that?"

"Joey on my soccer team said Mom should stay locked up because she did a bad thing."

Apparently something the kid overheard from his parents. Ian tightened his grip on his keys as he took in Griffin's slumped shoulders.

How many times did he get hassled by his friends but didn't say anything?

Ian ruffled Griffin's hair. "How'd that make you feel to hear people talk about your mom like that?"

"It made my stomach hurt." He wrapped his arms around his middle.

"Yeah, mine, too. The thing is, Bubba, your mom made a mistake, but you know she's facing the consequences. When the judge releases her, she will be home again."

"What if she has to go back to jail?"

"We're going to make sure she doesn't. You with me?" Ian held out his fist.

Griffin bumped knuckles with him, then splayed his fingers, making an explosion sound. "Yeah!"

"Why isn't Grandpa helping fix up this house? I heard him talking to Agnes when she came to the cabin. Doesn't he like Mom anymore?"

Ian rested an elbow on the window frame and rubbed a hand over his chin. What he was thinking couldn't be shared with his nephew, but he wasn't going to brush it aside as if things were fine with Dad.... The kid deserved a somewhat honest response.

"Grandpa is sad and angry about choices your mom had made. He needs to work things out in his own way."

"Grandma's sad, too. I see her cry sometimes. That makes my stomach hurt, too."

"I know, mine, too. Let's go inside and let Red know

we're here. Maybe you can show me anything that needs to be fixed."

"Like the way you fixed Grandma's kitchen sink and water shot to the ceiling?" Griffin grinned, revealing a gap in his front teeth.

Ian looped an arm around his neck and rubbed his knuckles playfully across the top of his head. "Whose side are you on anyway?"

Griffin squirmed out of Ian's grasp and reached for the ball on the floor by his feet. "Can I stay outside and play with my soccer ball?"

"Keep it away from the road and out of neighbors' yards."

"Okay." Griffin dropped the ball in the grass next to the driveway and started dribbling across the yard.

Snatching his phone off the seat, Ian exited his vehicle and headed for the house once he knew Griffin was fine.

As he opened the front door, the citrus scent of cleaner filled the air, replacing the musty smell that had greeted him in the past.

Red's voice bounced off the walls as she belted out the words to a familiar country song. Her voice, low and throaty, washed over him, releasing a longing in him.

He lounged against the doorjamb watching her dip her hips and shimmy her shoulders as she scrubbed the wall. "So this is the secret to your cleaning and brainstorming decorating ideas?"

She jumped, tugged on her earbuds and spun around. Pink crawled up her neck and colored her cheeks. "I didn't hear you come in."

"Obviously. Nice song. You have a great voice."

"I can't sing." She dropped her rag in the bucket and dried her hands on her shorts.

"Says who?"

She looked away and picked up her bucket.

"Right. Well, Bobby's an idiot. Listen to someone whose vote counts."

The door slammed, and then footsteps pounded across the floor. Griffin stomped into the room, his chest jerking with staggered breaths as he spoke. "I didn't mean to do it. Honest. It was an accident." He plopped down on the bottom step of the staircase and buried his face in his arms.

Ian and Red exchanged glances; then Ian walked to the stairs and sat beside him. "What's going on, Bubba?"

Tears streaked his freckled face when he raised his head. "That lady across the street is mean. I told her it was an accident, but she just started yelling."

That lady across the street had to be Evelyn Parnell, sister to Shelby Lake police chief Patrick Laughton, but she was also the first and loudest to speak out against Agape House.

Ian rubbed a hand over his forehead. This was a complication they didn't need. "How about if you tell me what happened?"

Before Griffin could speak, someone pounded on the front door. Ian didn't need two guesses about who was there.

Ian strode to the front door and opened it. Evelyn Parnell stood on the front step with thunder in her eyes. Lines deepened across her forehead and around her mouth. "Mrs. Parnell. How are you?"

She tugged on the jacket to her gray pantsuit and sniffed. "I was just fine until that little brat nephew of yours destroyed my flower bed."

Red appeared beside Ian. "Mrs. Parnell, lovely to see you."

The woman glared at the two of them over the rim of her glasses. "Is it?"

"Mrs. Parnell, what is it you think Griffin did?"

"He kicked his ball into my yard, smashing the celestial globe in my front flower bed." She waved a hand toward her house across the street.

Celestial globe? One of those colored gazing ball things?

Ian called over his shoulder, "Hey, Bubba, come here a minute."

Griffin trudged to the door, his head down and hands shoved in the pockets of his cargo shorts.

Ian kneeled in front of him and rested his hands on the kid's shoulders. "Did you break something of Mrs. Parnell's?"

"Yes, but I told her it was an accident."

"Did you apologize?"

"No."

"Think you should?"

"I'm sorry for breaking your ball thing, Mrs. Parnell." Griffin looked at Mrs. Parnell, then dropped his gaze to his feet and mumbled, "I will buy you a new one."

"That one was special and can't be replaced. Stay away from my yard. I don't have time for troublemakers like you." She turned on her heel and started down the sidewalk.

Red pulled Griffin against her and wrapped her arms around him. Hearing the kid's sniffles sent Ian's blood pressure rising.

Ian ground his teeth to keep from spitting out the words burning his tongue. He pushed past Red and stepped outside, closing the door. "Mrs. Parnell, my nephew is not a troublemaker. What happened was an accident, and he offered to replace it. Cut him some slack."

She whirled and shook her finger at him, her mouth pinched and eyebrows tugged together. "I'd expect a comment like that from you." She waved a hand across the front of the house. "Is that what you're planning to do with this abomination? Excuse their actions and tell the town to cut them some slack?"

"Griffin's actions weren't deliberate. Like I said, he apologized and offered to replace it. What more do you want?"

"What I want is for your family to take your business elsewhere…off my street and out of this town. I've already written letters to the parole board and the city council, voicing my displeasure. I haven't decided if I should send them or not."

His stomach tightened as his nerves thrummed. "That is your right, but I'm asking you to reconsider."

"Why should I do that?" She crossed her arms over her chest.

"This project affects many people—children like my nephew who need their parents out of prison and back in their lives. Parents, siblings, spouses…it's an opportunity to restore families."

His patience was wearing thin. He needed to end this conversation and leave before he said something he would regret—something that would jeopardize Agape House even further. He scoured his hands over his face.

His biggest fear about people like Evelyn Parnell—and surely she wasn't the only one in the community who felt this way—was them approaching his sister while she lived at Agape House. Would she have the strength to stick it out, or would she try to run?

"We want to show Christ-like love to others and offer a second chance at life. Isn't that what being a Christian is all about?"

"Don't you preach to me about being a Christian. I've been in the church longer than you've been alive, young man."

"Being in church doesn't make one a Christian. Again, I'm sorry on Griffin's behalf about the celestial ball thing. I'll do some research and send you a check to replace it."

Ian stalked back into the house and slammed the door. He forced himself to relax so he didn't vent his frustration in front of Griffin.

He returned to the living room to find Red and Griffin sitting together on the bottom step. The boy looked up.

"Uncle Ian, I'm sorry for being a troublemaker."

Ian knelt in front of the kid and ruffled his hair. "Bubba, you're not a troublemaker. It was an accident. Next time kick your soccer ball in the backyard. Let's get some grub. Where do you want to go?"

"Can we have tacos?"

"Works for me." Ian held out a fist and bumped knuckles with Griffin.

He'd lost any appetite he had, but he needed to get away from Agape House and find a quiet place to think and pray and beg God not to allow those letters to be mailed.

Chapter Seven

A month ago, if anyone had told Agnes she'd be moving back home, she'd say they were off their rocker.

But here she was—flipping ribs on Mama's deck and painting them with Memaw's barbecue sauce recipe. The meat sizzled against the cast-iron grates. Smoke tangled with the scent of barbecue and drifted through the air to whet the appetites of her guests.

Leaving her apartment had been bittersweet, but having Ian, Josie, Nick, Lindsey and Stephen help move her stuff into Mama's garage eased the ache a little. She couldn't do it herself, and knowing she had friends she could count on…well, that just made her heart sweeter than sugar.

Ian and Josie continued to remind her God had something greater in store for her.

She hoped they were right.

Spending the next two months or so without paying rent should have straightened the twists in her stomach, but if she didn't have enough money for the down payment on the cottage, then she'd have to figure out new living arrangements.

She couldn't dwell on that now. She had a yard full of

people to feed, and no one wanted to listen to her belly-aching.

Grabbing the barbecue brush again, she mopped more sauce across the boneless ribs and closed the lid on the grill. She slid the glass patio door open and headed for the kitchen.

"Take these drinks to the table, darlin'." Mama handed her pitchers of sweet tea and lemonade.

"The ribs are about ready to fall off the bone."

"All righty, then. Send those kids in here to wash up."

And by kids, Mama meant anyone under the age of forty.

Carrying the beverages to the deck, she glanced across the yard where Hannah kept the younger kids entertained with bottles of bubbles.

A shout from the yard drew her attention to where the others played cornhole. Josie did a victory dance with her hands punching the air. Shaking his head and laughing, Nick retrieved the corn-filled bags and handed them back to her.

Stephen and Lindsey's eighteen-month-old daughter, Gracie Ann, left her friends and toddled over to her daddy. Before Stephen could pick her up, Ian swooped down, grabbed her and gave her a gentle toss in the air before catching her safely. She giggled and begged for him to do it again.

The relaxed expression on his face warmed her from the inside out. He needed to marry a good woman and raise his own family. He'd dated through the years, but had never hinted about settling down. Not even with Emily. Though thinking back on seeing Ian with his ex, caused Agnes's stomach to ache. Just like it always had.

If only she could be the one to make him happy. If she

could give him what he needed, then she'd take Josie's advice and go for it.

The patio door slid open, pulling Agnes out of her thoughts and back to the barbecue.

Mama carried out two blue glass bowls, one filled with potato salad and the other mounded with coleslaw. "Agnes Joy, grab the pinto beans and macaroni and cheese off the stove please?"

Favorites from her childhood. And what better way to host a picnic than to share with her closest friends?

"Sure thing, Mama."

"Okay, looks like everything's set." Casting a glance over the laden table, Mama pressed her pinkies to the corners of her mouth and whistled, catching everyone's attention. She waved them toward the deck. "Food's ready. Let's wash up and eat!"

Stephen and Lindsey's baby son, Thomas, squalled from his carrier in the shaded corner of the deck at the sound of Mama's raised voice.

Mama unbuckled him, lifted his tiny body and cradled him against her chest. "So sorry, little man, did I disrupt your nap?"

The kids raced for the deck and thundered up the steps, only to be stopped by Mama, who directed them to the kitchen sink like a drill instructor, only with a sweeter smile.

Having traded Gracie Ann for Josie's son, Noah, Ian led the way with the child clutching his thumb as they walked slowly to the deck.

A longing as gentle as the afternoon breeze whispered across her heart. Agnes sighed.

Ian buckled Noah into his portable high chair, then wandered over to her as she plated the ribs. He put his hands on her upper arms and looked over her shoulder into the grill. "Spread looks good, Red."

His presence created more warmth than the open grill heating her face and neck. The scent of his cologne caused her to toes curl. She wanted to lean into him, to be captured by his embrace and allow the moments in time to stand still while she savored his closeness.

Swallowing a couple of times, she nudged him back with her elbow and handed him the platter. "Set this on the table please. It's mostly Mama's doing. As soon as the kids get settled and someone blesses the food, we can eat."

Life would be so much simpler if her heart didn't over-react every time the guy came within a three-foot radius of her personal space. But ever since she'd brushed that kiss across his lips… Once the kids returned to the deck with somewhat clean hands, everyone moved into a circle. Sandwiched between Hannah and Ian, she grabbed his outstretched hand, his rough palm warm against hers.

They bowed their heads while Mama prayed.

Once Mama concluded with amen, Ian gave Agnes's hand a gentle squeeze. For a second, she focused on the way his fingers entwined with hers, the heat of his skin and the gentleness of his touch. She imagined how it would be to have that kind of relationship with him. Just for a second…

Noah yelped, returning her attention back to the present.

What was wrong with her?

She pulled her hand out of his grip and wiped it on her capris, then held up her arms to get everyone's attention. "Before we raid this feast like ants at a picnic, I just wanted to say thanks for today. All y'all's support and help means a lot."

"Moving all that furniture was worth it for this Texas barbecue, Red." Ian picked up a paper plate and fanned Noah's face, causing the little one to giggle.

Once everyone was settled, Agnes set her full plate across from Ian.

Laughter and raised voices drifted over the treetops as everyone talked over everyone else. Mama's house was meant to be filled with people. It was much too big to be wasted on one or two people. They had hoped for grandchildren one day.

If only…

"You okay?" Ian glanced at her from across the table. Sunlight glinted off the top of his head, turning his sandy-brown tousled hair almost white.

"Just dandy. Need anything?"

He wiped a smear of sauce off his mouth. "I'm good. I may need a nap after this feast…or maybe a walk to burn off the calories."

"Calories have never been your problem, Ian."

"Is that so?" Puffing his chest and patting his flat stomach, he waggled his eyebrows, sending a surge of heat across Agnes's cheeks.

She took another drink of tea, suddenly feeling parched, then stood and carried her nearly empty plate into the kitchen.

What was her problem? She needed to get a grip.

After all, she was going to be next door to the guy for the summer and couldn't act like a fifteen-year-old every time they were together.

She ran water into the sink and added a squirt of dish soap.

The patio door slid open. Josie entered the kitchen carrying a stack of paper plates. "You left the table in a hurry. Everything okay?"

Agnes took the paper plates from her and dropped them in the trash. "Yes."

"Agnes...what's going on?"

"Nothing. I'm fine." She wrung out the sponge and moved to the stove, scrubbing the top clean enough to win Mama's seal of approval.

Josie plunged her hands in the dishwater and scrubbed Mama's favorite bean pot. "Every time Ian comes near you, you practically jump out your skin."

And almost into his arms.

"I told you—I'm fine."

"I've seen how he's been watching you all day. He can't take his eyes off you." After rinsing the dishes, she dried her hands and targeted Agnes with a direct look.

Not Ian.

"He just wanted to be sure I wasn't burning the ribs."

"I doubt it. It's more than that—the guy looks at you like a man in love. What do you say about taking a wrecking ball to that wall around your heart and giving the guy a chance?"

"He doesn't want me, Sugar Pie. He made it clear years ago we were nothing more than friends." Agnes leaned against the fridge, resting her shoulder against the cool stainless steel. "Ian and I are just friends. In fact, if Ian's moved on from Emily, I have half a mind to fix him up with Breena Nelson—she'd be just his type."

Breena was a regular at Cuppa Josie's who owned a clothing boutique down the street from the coffee shop.

"No way. Ian wants a woman of substance. Breena's sweet and cute, but her conversational skills rarely venture past fashion. I can't see Ian talking about styles and colors."

"Well, there's got to be a woman out there for him.

The guy's been dragging his feet about finding his own wife, and let's face it—he isn't getting any younger."

Wasn't that what friends did for one another—look out for their interests? If so, then why did the idea of Ian dating someone else make her heart mourn?

He didn't want Red playing matchmaker—he wanted her.

Crazy woman. What did he have to do to get that through her head?

Ian counted to twenty before pushing through the sliding glass door. He didn't mean to eavesdrop, but maybe they didn't realize the window over the kitchen sink was open. And he heard every word of her conversation with Josie.

Every heart-stabbing word.

Most guys would probably consider him an idiot for pining over the one woman he couldn't have, but when he dated other women, he kept measuring them against Red's yardstick. Not fair to them or Red, but that's how it was.

And Mom's subtle hints about more grandchildren haven't gone unnoticed. With forty only a couple of years away, he needed to up his game if he was going to have children and be able to keep up with them without a wheelchair and an oxygen tank.

Did men have biological clocks?

He loved kids and wanted his own, but only with Red.

And she kept him firmly in the friend zone.

He carried the nearly empty platter of ribs and set it on the counter. "Toss me a cloth, Red, and I'll wipe down the tables for you."

Josie glanced at him, at Red, then at the open window. Red wrung out a red plaid dishcloth and tossed it to him. He caught it one-handed and pivoted to head back to the deck.

Josie followed. "Ian, you got a minute?"

Ian glanced over his shoulder at the open window above the sink. He dropped the cloth on the table. "Sure."

They left the deck and headed toward the koi pond. Ian shoved his hands in the front pockets of his jeans. "What's up?"

Josie folded her arms in front of her. "I didn't realize the window was open until you came into the kitchen. I'm going to assume you heard our conversation."

"Yeah." He watched a dragonfly flit from one yellow flower to another.

"I'm sorry if I was out of line with anything I said."

"Don't sweat it."

"You're in love with her, aren't you?"

Ian shaded his eyes against the sun and looked at her, wishing he had grabbed his sunglasses off the picnic table. "Are you always this direct?"

"Only with people I care about. I care about Agnes. Her ex did a number on her."

He didn't need to be reminded. "Yeah, I know."

Josie sat on the stone pond wall and looked at him. She pulled on a long blade of grass and wove it through her fingers. "You're welcome to tell me to mind my own business, but *are* you in love with Agnes?"

"Why do you ask?"

"I just don't want to see her hurt again."

"Believe me, I'm the last guy who'd ever hurt her." Ian looked over his shoulder to find Red running barefoot in the grass chasing Gracie Ann and Noah. Her laughter swirled with their giggles and zeroed in on his heart.

"Hurt comes in many forms, my friend."

Ian turned back to Josie. "Like I said—you don't have to worry about me."

"I guess what I'm saying is if you do love her, maybe now's the time to start showing her."

She was right. He needed to show Red just how great they'd be together, but he wasn't sure how to do that without spooking her...or worse, driving her away for good.

Ian focused his attention on the fat orange and white fish playing tag. "So, if a guy wanted to move out of the friend zone, what would you suggest he do?"

"I'm going to break girl code and let you in on a secret, but it's because you're both driving me nuts with the way you're refusing to talk about the one thing keeping you apart—your relationship. Agnes thinks you see her only as a friend. If you want her heart, then woo her and show her how much you care."

He didn't want to do a bunch of meaningless actions to get her attention. He wanted her to know he was the right man for her...for the rest of their lives.

Chapter Eight

One man's trash was another man's treasure. Or in her case, another woman's treasure.

Agnes's eyes swept over the front yard littered with mismatched furniture and tables of household goods. The estate sale offered promise. Hopefully she could find something to restore for Agape House.

At the sound of a car door closing behind her, Agnes turned and pushed her oversize sunglasses on top of her head.

Ian climbed out of his white Ford Escape parked behind her convertible. He smothered a yawn, then finger-combed his damp hair away from his face.

She handed him a steaming Cuppa Josie's cup and smiled. "Mornin', Sunshine."

He removed the lid and breathed deeply. "What flavor? Actually, it doesn't matter as long as it's caffeine."

"Drink your coffee, and wipe the cobwebs from your eyes."

"Red, why does every harebrained idea of yours have to happen this side of seven o'clock? You know it's Saturday, right?" The morning sunshine streamed through the stocky sycamore tree, casting leaf-shaped shadows on his face.

"Hey, Mr. Cranky Pants, when I mentioned going to yard sales this morning, you're the one who offered to come with me. Just because you think morning begins at ten, some of us have things to do. The best deals are found first thing before everything is picked over like a stewed chicken."

"Speaking of chickens—if you lived on a farm, you'd be kicking the rooster awake." Creases puckered the corners of his eyes, showing laughter fit him as well as his faded jeans.

Why was she checking out his jeans?

She tugged on the hem of her fitted pink T-shirt and nodded toward the small crowd rooting through the tables. "The buzzards started circling before dawn."

"Aren't you one of those buzzards?"

"No way, I'm much cuter." She bumped her shoulder against his.

"You're right about that." He waggled his eyebrows over the rim of his cup.

Agnes rolled her eyes.

Ian stretched his arms out in a wide *Y* before smothering another yawn, causing his untucked green pinstriped button-down shirt to ride up. "Okay, Red, what's the game plan?"

"We're on a treasure hunt for Agape House."

"That thrift store explosion in your mom's garage isn't enough?" He tugged on her ponytail. "You're a sucker for a lost cause, aren't you?"

"Lost cause, my foot. Repurposing furniture keeps us in line with your precious budget. Plus, the more we display at Agape House, the more advertising for Tattered Daisies." She poked his chest. "Don't be dissin' my dream."

"I wasn't." He swept a hand across the yard. "Face it—some of this stuff looks like junk."

"You see junk—I see potential for a second chance. With a little TLC, these pieces can have value again."

"Kind of like a mouthy redhead I know. Okay, let's do this. If I'm going to be your muscles, better use them while they're fresh." Ian flexed his biceps.

Agnes tried not to notice the bulge that tightened against the cotton fabric of his shirt. For a geek, he did have some strong arms. Not that she'd dare admit that to him…or anyone.

Squinting, she leaned close to his arm and poked his upper arm. "Hmm, maybe I should've called someone else."

"No respect, I tell you." He pulled his sunglasses out of his front pocket and settled them on his nose.

Agnes looped her hand through the crook of his elbow and guided him toward the sale.

A dented toaster, a Crock-Pot without a lid, mismatched coffee mugs, grungy linens, musty books and faded toys waited to be chosen. Every item had a history, some tie to the past. And now they sat in the early morning sunshine waiting for someone else to give them new life.

Agnes leafed through an old Fannie Farmer cookbook. Maybe Josie would like this. "Why haven't you called Breena yet? I gave you her number last week after the barbecue."

"Forget it, Red. I can find my own dates." Ian leafed through a book on basement remodeling, the pictures suggesting a mid-'70s copyright date.

"Well, you're not doing a very good job at it." She

dropped the cookbook on the pile and headed for a small pedestal table marred with water rings. She ran a hand over the scarred top and imagined it repainted a light aqua—maybe with chalk paint—and holding trailing ivy. Or a cup of tea. Perfect for a small reading table.

"What's that supposed to mean?" He grabbed her hand as she searched the table for a price tag.

"You're a great guy, Ian. Any girl would be lucky to lasso you."

"I'm not a rodeo steer. Besides, I'm not looking for just any girl." The pad of his thumb caressed the inside of her wrist. Almost a whisper of a touch. He gave her a slow smile, revealing white teeth, and winked. At her.

Ian James *winked* at her.

The fool must've had an eye twitch or something. Why would he do such a thing?

Gently she pulled her hand away and rubbed at the warmth flowing to her shoulder. Stifling a shiver, she picked up the table to check for a price tag. "Leave it to me—I'll fix you up with the perfect girl."

"How about a sassy, ginger-haired transplanted Texan?"

Agnes's heart shimmied. Must be too much caffeine. "That makes about as much sense as hip pockets on a hog. You don't want a throwaway whose heart has more dents than a junkyard wreck."

Ian tipped up her chin and leveled her with a direct look. "He really did a number on you."

"I don't know what you're talking about." Agnes pulled her gaze away from Ian's insightful stare.

He scoffed. "Right. You go on believing that."

Forgetting the table a moment, Agnes crossed her arms over her chest. "Ian James, I know who I am."

His voice lost its teasing tone, and a look of compassion brushed across his face. "No, Red, you don't. You've been poisoned by his decade of lies. It's time you listened to the truth about yourself."

Tired of their conversation, she pointed at a dresser near the front porch. "I'm going to check out that dresser. Be right back."

Agnes hurried across the yard without waiting to see if Ian followed. At times, his probing touched on those tender spots her emotional armor couldn't quite cover.

A ripped piece of cardboard with FREE scrawled in black marker had been duct-taped to one of the drawers.

Free—definitely in her price range.

She ran her hands over the curved edges of the tall highboy with its six drawers, missing handles and beaten exterior. Why hadn't anyone claimed this beauty?

Sanded down with a fresh coat of paint and a varnished top, this dresser would be a nice addition to one of the bedrooms at Agape House. It still had potential, yet it had been set out with the rest of the unwanted stuff.

Discarded. Without value. Oh, how she understood that.

But not anymore.

She'd take this baby home and turn someone else's trash into her treasure. She patted the top of the dresser and nodded toward his SUV. "Think you can put that muscle to good use and help me get this dresser home?"

"Sure."

While Ian jogged to his truck to open the back, Agnes tilted the dresser, then started dragging it across the grass, the dew dampening her sandaled feet.

Ian stopped her and reached for the dresser. "Hey, let me get that."

"Why? You think little ole me can't handle such a manly job?"

"This has nothing to do with your size or your abilities." Stooping, Ian hugged the dresser frame and carried it to his vehicle. The thin material of his shirt did little to disguise the flexed muscles in his back. He set it on the road and smiled. "Just let me be a gentleman, okay?"

"I can help you get it in there." She reached for the side of the dresser.

Ian pushed her hand away. "No need."

"I insist."

"I got it, Red." He edged the top of the dresser into the back of his SUV. Agnes grabbed the right legs while he navigated the left side.

He stopped. "Wait a minute. It's caught."

"What?" Agnes pushed her side in.

"Stop!"

The right side kicked up like a frisky calf. The front dresser leg scraped across Agnes's cheekbone. The bottom leg cracked her in the jaw, snapping her teeth together.

Pain exploded down the side of her face, stealing her breath. Cupping her hands over her cheek, she stumbled backward, tripping over the curb and falling against a tree. She grazed her shoulder against the rough tree bark.

Sticky wetness trickled between her fingers.

Ian dropped on the grass beside her. "You're bleeding."

"Very astute, Sherlock." She glared at him with her good eye.

"Let me see." He peeled her hands away and sucked air between clenched teeth.

Agnes tried not to wince as he brushed her hair out the way and probed her face.

"You have a small cut, but I don't think it's deep enough for stitches. Your face is swelling. Sit tight while I grab my first aid kit."

Where else would she go? Sprint to her car and drive off? Not likely.

Ian returned with a blue and red zippered bag.

"You're such a Boy Scout."

He tore open an antiseptic wipe and dabbed at the wound. She forced a sharp hiss between her teeth and curled her fingers into the cool blades of grass.

He stroked her cheek with his thumb. "Sorry. Want me to stop?"

"No, just don't be taking your sweet time about it."

Ian finished his torture and pasted a couple of bandages below her eye. He smacked a plastic pouch on his knee and pressed it to her jaw, the cold calming the throbbing pain.

She rested her head against the tree, not caring the rough bark would tangle her hair into a bird's nest by the time she stood.

Inches from her face, his eyes sparked. She wanted to rub a thumb across his forehead to erase the puckered frown. Instead she took in the bump on the bridge of his nose, the hint of shadow across the angle of his jaw and the scar on his chin from the time she pushed him off the dock when he was thirteen. His lips parted slightly.

If she leaned forward an inch or two, she could kiss…

She jerked her head back, smacking it on the tree trunk. She clamped back a cry. That dresser must've cracked more than her face. Like her common sense.

She had to stop thinking about kissing Ian.

Otherwise she was going to end up heartbroken when she couldn't give him what he truly wanted.

Nothing like knocking a lady in the face with a dresser to show how much he cares.

Ian dragged his gaze away from Red's swollen face

where a bruise pooled under her pale skin. He focused on the freckles sprinkled across her nose. He gathered the trash and first aid kit and dropped everything on the passenger seat of his Escape. Otherwise he was going to cradle her face and kiss away the pain from her injuries.

Calling himself all kinds of stupid, he headed to the back of the SUV to free up the dresser caught on the gray interior carpeting and closed the liftgate.

He walked back to the tree and dropped to the ground, wrapping his arms around his knees. "All loaded. How about if I give you a ride home, then come back for your car?"

She slid her feet into those ridiculous pink high-heeled sandals, dusted off her jeans and handed him the cold compress. Her riot of red curls escaped the tamed ponytail and formed corkscrews around her ears. "I can drive home."

Ian jumped up and jammed his hands in his front pockets to keep from running his fingers through her wild hair. "You sure?"

"I appreciate your help and all, but you don't need to baby me. Now let's get that chest of drawers home so I can start working on it." She walked to her car, threw a glance over her shoulder, then slid behind the wheel and started the engine.

Crazy, independent woman.

Short of throwing Red over his shoulder and locking her in his car, he had no choice but to follow her.

Less than ten minutes later, Red pulled into her mother's driveway and shut off the engine. Ian parked behind her, slid out from behind the steering wheel and released the liftgate. He pulled the dresser out of its tight quarters and carried it into the garage, setting it next to a chair with torn upholstery.

Red smoothed her hair into a ponytail and secured it with her hair band, exposing her cheek.

He gently touched her skin. "That's going to leave a nasty bruise. Man, I'm so sorry."

She pushed his hand away. "Would you stop? It was an accident. The bruises will fade. I'll be just fine."

Talking from experience?

After knowing more about her past with Bobby, Ian felt his gut burning to think he could mar her beautiful skin as that jerk did.

It'd been an accident, but he still wanted to make her feel better. "How about a movie and popcorn tonight?"

"A movie of my choosing?"

"You pick the movie, I'll bring the popcorn."

If his instincts were right, Red would want some chick flick. Any other time he'd rather gouge his eyes out with a fork than spend ninety minutes watching a movie that kept the guy and girl apart until the end. But they didn't call them chick flicks for nothing.

Maybe the movie with dimmed lighting and space for two on her mother's couch would soften her heart and see him in a new light.

His cell phone rang. He fished it out of his front pocket and caught Mom's cell number on the screen. "Hey, Mom. What's up?"

"Where are you, Ian?" Her voice sounded tight.

He turned in the direction of his parents' house. "I'm next door with Red. Why?"

"Chief Laughton's here and wants to talk to us."

"Why?" His hand tightened around the phone.

"He hasn't said yet."

"I'll be right there." Ian ended the call and clutched the phone in his fist. He scrubbed a hand over his face and sighed.

"What's wrong?"

"Chief Laughton is at the house and wants to talk to all of us. I need to head home for a bit."

"Being one of your daddy's oldest friends, the chief's been at your house plenty of times."

"Yeah, but I don't think this is a social call." He shrugged, trying not to jump to conclusions. "I don't know."

"Want me to come?"

Ian eyed her bruised face and shook his head. No need to draw anyone's attention to his stupidity. "I'll be fine. You take it easy, and I'll be back in a bit."

"Let me know if you need me." She laid a hand on his forearm.

"I will." He leaned forward and almost brushed a kiss across her lips until he glimpsed her wide-eyed stare. He dropped a quick kiss on her brow by the wound.

Way to go, idiot.

He needed to get a grip before she decked him for taking advantage. Then they'd both be sporting bruises.

Ian slid behind the steering wheel, backed out of the driveway and parked in front of his parents' house next to Chief Laughton's black sedan.

He strode through the back door and into the living room. Mom sat on the edge of her chair like a nervous bunny, twisting her wedding band. Chief Laughton lounged on the couch, right foot resting on his left knee, and held a cup of coffee.

Upon seeing Ian, the chief set his cup on the coffee table, rose and extended his hand. "Ian. Good to see you."

Ian gripped the older man's hand. "Why do I get the feeling this isn't a social call? You know Dad's at the cabin, right?"

Did something else happen with Griffin? The kid had

been a little subdued since the incident with the soccer ball last week.

Chief Laughton held up a hand. "No need to worry. This isn't official police business."

Ian shot a glance at Mom. "Where's Griffin?"

"He's next door at Jimmy's watching a movie."

"Okay, good." Ian crossed his arms over his chest. "So, what's up, Chief?"

Chief Laughton shoved his hands in the front pockets of his jeans and jingled his change. "My sister, Evelyn, came to see me yesterday. Apparently the two of you exchanged words the other day?"

Ian nodded. "Yes, sir. About a week and a half ago."

"What happened, Ian?"

Ian gestured for the chief to have a seat, then retold the incident with Mrs. Parnell, ending with her threat to send her letters to the parole board and the city council.

The chief tugged on his pant legs, then sat and reached for his coffee cup. "Evelyn insists I do something to shut down Agape House."

"You can't do that." The color drained from Mom's face. "I mean, we need—"

The chief held up a hand again. "No worries, Charlotte. You've done everything by the book to get this program going. And I, for one, admire and respect what you're doing."

"Then what's the problem?" Mom relaxed slightly and clasped her hands in her lap.

"Although her son was killed almost twenty years ago by a drunk driver, living across the street and watching the restoration process on the Miller estate reopens a very painful time for Evelyn. I don't have to remind you how vocal she was about Zoe's sentencing."

"Patrick, I remember when your nephew was killed.

I'm so sorry for what Evelyn went through—what your family went through—but Zoe is serving out her sentence."

"I understand that, but soon you'll have a chance to have her home again. Evelyn doesn't have that option."

Mom walked to the fireplace and picked up Zoe's senior picture. She ran a hand over the glass. "What she did was wrong, but I just want my daughter to have a chance to start over, make something of her life. Isn't that worth something?" Her voice caught, almost pleading.

Ian ground his teeth together, turning away from looking at Mom. Seeing her upset tore up his insides.

Chief Laughton rose to his feet and puffed out his barrel chest. He ran a hand over his short graying hair. "It's worth quite a lot actually. During my law enforcement career, I've seen it all. Nothing really surprises me anymore. I guess it's made an old cynic out of me. I want to believe Agape House will change those women's lives, helping them rise above their mistakes and adjust back into society. I will continue to support your efforts, Charlotte."

"Then why are you here?" Ian didn't mean for his words to come out so abruptly, but he couldn't take back the tone now.

Chief sighed and laid a hand on Ian's shoulder. "I'm caught between duty and family. If Agape House can help prevent other families from struggling with the same grief, then I'm not going to stand in your way. But, as a big brother, I'm asking you to be understanding of my sister's feelings as she tries to come to terms with this program. I'm praying once she sees how it benefits the community, she'll have a change of heart."

He wasn't the only one. They didn't need resistance to getting Agape House up and running. Every day falling off the calendar felt like another tick of a bomb, and if Ian could help it, he'd do everything in his power to keep this from blowing up in their faces.

"Thank you for sharing your concern, Patrick. We will be mindful of Evelyn as we're working on Agape House."

"And that's all I ask. Thanks for your time."

Mom walked Chief Laughton to the door, then strode back into the living room.

"Mom, her actions are ridiculous."

Mom picked up Chief Laughton's empty coffee cup. "To us, maybe, but she's hurting, Ian. From what I understand, Evelyn never allowed herself to grieve properly after losing her son. We can't control what she does, but we can control how we react. Let's focus on extending grace and leaving the rest to God."

Mom, the veritable fount of wisdom.

Her faith brought his to shame.

If the roles were reversed, maybe he'd be crusading like Evelyn Parnell to keep Agape House from opening, too.

He sighed and kneaded his temples to massage away building pain. There had to be a way to find a compromise in this situation. Right now he couldn't see what it was. And that ate at his stomach like battery acid.

Chapter Nine

Agnes tried to relax. Really, she did.

With her hands tucked behind her head, she lay on the plaid blanket next to a napping Noah while Josie threw horseshoes with Nick and Ian.

Above her head, birds flittered from branch to branch. She envied their freedom. Patches of sunshine soaked into her skin as she listened to laughter curling in the afternoon breeze that ruffled the stray pieces of hair around her face.

As hard as she tried to enjoy the lingering scent of grilled hamburgers, the clink of horseshoes against the stakes and the squeals of little kids running around the playground, her muscles remained tense.

Agnes scanned the families spread out on blankets in the grass, huddled in discussions at the picnic tables under the pavilion and playing on the playground or at the basketball court.

She loved the Shelby Lake Community Church annual picnic held the Saturday before Father's Day. What wasn't to love about potluck, games and hanging out with friends? But right now she struggled with having a good time with the open house nipping at their heels like a frisky pup.

Had it been six weeks since Ian asked her for help with Agape House?

Instead of enjoying the afternoon, she couldn't shut off the mental ticking of jobs on her to-do list.

Accent tables and a dresser had been sanded but needed a base coat of paint. She had spent last night sewing throw pillows for the living room, but the club chairs still needed to be stripped and reupholstered.

At Agape House, the downstairs was coming along, thanks to the groups of volunteers, but she hadn't even touched the upstairs. Her chest still tightened when she just thought about climbing those steps.

When Ian wasn't working on claims or at Agape House, they spent evenings sitting on the dock, watching movies or rowing across the lake.

Every day she fell deeper in love with her best friend. And that scared her more than a bagful of rattlesnakes. She needed to face reality—she wasn't the right woman for Ian. By prolonging the inevitable, she was setting her heart up for destruction.

A shadow fell over the blanket. Agnes shielded her eyes and looked up to find Ian standing over her, threading a blue bandanna between his fingers.

Dressed in an untucked white button-down with cuffs rolled to his sleeves, exposing his strong forearms, and khaki cargo shorts, Ian embodied casual.

She tried not to dwell on his muscular calves inches from her face—calves she's seen thousands of times over the years—and kept her gaze locked with his. That way she could ignore the unexpected flutter in her stomach.

He dropped to his haunches and lowered his voice. "So, you wanna do the three-legged race with me?"

"I don't think so." She rose to her elbows.

"Why not?"

"I like not walking around on crutches?" *Crazy man.* "Besides, I'm keeping an eye on Noah while he's napping."

"You're not going to break a leg. Teamwork's the key—we seem to do pretty well in that department. And Josie said she'd be right over to relieve you if you said yes. They're about finished with their game."

She pondered it a moment and accepted the wisdom of his words—they did make a great team, especially when he agreed with her. "Okay, fine, but if anything happens, you'll be at my beck and call until I'm off crutches."

"You got it. Let's go." He offered a hand.

She placed hers in his and nearly fell back to the blanket by the shock skimming her skin. Jumping up, she stuffed her feet in her platform wedges, called to Josie to let her know where she was going and crossed the field by his side.

Ian stopped her and pointed to her feet. "There's no way you're going to race in those crazy shoes."

"These shoes aren't crazy. I bought them on sale."

"How are you at running barefoot?"

"About as good as your nephew charming cookies from his grandma." Agnes pointed to Griffin running off with a cookie in both hands, taking bites as he met up with his friends.

Ian laughed, the sound flowing over Agnes's soul like melted caramel. "That good, huh?"

They reached the rest of the racers. Agnes kicked off her shoes and joined Ian at the starting line.

"Put your leg against mine." He slapped the side of his khaki shorts.

Ian leaned over and tied his right leg to her left. She

was glad she had chosen jeans after the cold front had come in yesterday and dosed them with a chilly shower. At least the sun brightened the sky for the picnic.

He stood and slung an arm around Agnes's shoulders. "Match my stride. Finish line is over by those trees." He pointed to the grove of pines near the pavilion.

They lined up behind the long strip of masking tape used as the starting line. She peered down the line to check out their competition. Only to realize they were the only unmarried, unattached coed couple. Several of her junior high students paired up with friends of the same sex. Lindsey and Stephen Chase coupled up. Nick and Hannah moved beside them.

The awareness of Ian's closeness feathered her skin. The heat of his arm against her neck. The strength of his touch. The scent of his cologne.

Maybe she had too much sun and needed to sit out the race. Yes, maybe that was it…too much sun.

She had to remember Ian could be her friend and nothing more.

"Maybe this isn't such a good idea." She reached down to untie their bandanna.

Ian covered her hand to stop her. "Why not?"

She jerked her head to the others. "We're the only coeds who aren't a couple."

"We can change that." Ian roped an arm around her waist and drew her close.

She pushed him away and swatted at him. "Would you be serious?"

He seared her with a look that stole her breath. "What makes you think I'm not?"

She placed a hand on her chest and forced air into her lungs.

He wasn't serious. Was he?

Before she could contemplate it further, Pastor Nathan stood in front of the group, holding his three-year-old son Nathanial's hand. "Nate's going to count to three and tell you when to go."

Nate peered out from under his daddy's oversize ball cap and held up his fingers. "One. Two. Three go!"

Pastor Nathan grabbed his son around the waist and ran to the sidelines to avoid getting trampled.

Ian pulled her close. "Come on, Red. Let's do this."

He was talking about the race, right?

Slipping an arm around his waist for balance, she matched his gait. Once they fell into the rhythm of half running, half walking together, it wasn't as difficult as she expected.

Shouts came from the gathered crowd. She jerked her head upon hearing her name. Someone was cheering for them?

She stumbled.

Ian pulled her to her feet. "Follow my lead, Red. We can do this."

"Why do I have to follow your lead? You can follow mine."

"My legs are longer." He grinned, then shifted his focus to the masking tape finish line.

"You're just more competitive."

They scuttled across the grass. Ian's fingers pressed into her waist, warming her skin through the fabric of her blouse.

Friends egged them to the finish. She realized they were in the lead. But, out of the corner of her eye, Agnes caught sight of Hannah and Nick gaining on them. She tugged on Ian's arm. "Slow down."

He slammed her with an incredulous look. "What? Are you kidding? We have this thing."

"There's more to winning than crossing the finish line, Ian. Slow down."

When he didn't listen, Agnes lurched forward, pretending to stumble, knocking Ian to his knees. He rolled and grabbed her by the waist so she wouldn't topple over him. They landed side by side in the grass. She winced as the bandanna tightened on her ankle.

"And you complained about *me* breaking your leg. What's up with that?"

Hannah released a whoop of joy as she and her daddy crossed the finish line.

Ian glanced at them, then at Agnes. "Oh…slow down."

She winked. "You're a quick one, Ian James."

"Why didn't you just say something?" He tapped the end of her nose.

"Duh. I did." Agnes struggled to untie the knot Ian had cinched around their ankles, hating the way her fingers trembled.

Finally releasing the fabric, she pulled it loose and dropped it on Ian's shoulder. She rose to her feet and dusted off her jeans. "I need a drink. Want anything?"

"Grab me something cold."

"Like what?"

"Whatever you're having is fine."

Agnes hurried across the grass, needing a few minutes to catch her breath.

As she passed behind the still-laden food tables, she heard her name and slowed upon recognizing Evelyn Parnell's shrill voice.

Since Chief Laughton's visit with Ian and Charlotte, they made an extra effort to stay out of her way.

She paused in the shadows as Evelyn stood at the food table with her sister, Iris, filling take-out containers. Their round shapes and salon-coiffed graying hair made it difficult to tell them apart from behind, but bitterness made hard edges and thin lines on Evelyn's face, while a quick smile and kind eyes softened Iris's features.

"I'm telling you, Iris—the way they carried on... embarrassing."

"Relax, Evelyn, it's only a game. Agnes and Ian have known each other for years. They're practically brother and sister."

Agnes nodded with Iris's statement, but what she had felt on the field was far from sisterly.

"Ian trails after her like a smitten puppy. Pathetic. They're together all the time at that house." Evelyn plopped another spoonful of something into one of the containers. "Oh, I hate that place. I wish it would burn to the ground."

Agnes bit back a gasp.

"What a terrible thing to say!" Iris scowled at Evelyn.

"I mean it, Iris. It's going to be filled with drunks and troublemakers." She punctuated the air with her spoon. "Mark my words."

"Charlotte James won't let that happen. I heard her speak at the women's club about the Agape project. She has a heart for those women."

"Then she should have tried harder to control her daughter. Then we wouldn't be plagued with that eyesore."

"Oh, Evelyn, deep down, you know Agape House is a great resource for this community."

"Those women have no business in our neighborhood. Even our brother turned against me, but I won't rest until that project is shut down. Did you hear Pete was staying at their cabin at the lake? Even behind bars, their daughter is still causing trouble."

Agnes's ears burned so hot she was afraid they'd catch

on fire. Mama always told her to stop and think before she said anything, but Mama was in Texas. Agnes wasn't about to let these so-called Christian women drag Ian's family through the mud.

She moved out of her shadow and walked up behind the two women. "Afternoon, ladies."

Spoon in hand, Evelyn whirled around, flinging macaroni salad in the grass. Her face colored brighter than the red plastic bowl that held the pasta. She shot a glance at her sister, then dropped her gaze to the salad in front of her. "Afternoon, Agnes."

Iris grabbed a napkin and cleaned up the spilled macaroni salad.

"You two should be sitting in the sunshine instead of under this dark pavilion."

"Someone needs to be doing the Lord's work and fixing meals for our shut-ins." Evelyn closed the box and reached for another. The screechy sound of the foam sent a shiver down Agnes's spine.

She reached for a baby carrot off a veggie tray. "Does the Lord's work consist of bashing thy neighbor?"

"It most certainly does not."

"Your ugly words are very damaging to people I love. Ian James is my best friend. His parents are two of the kindest people I know. Everyone deserves a second chance, don't you think?"

"You don't know what it's like to have your baby taken from you, so don't stand there with your righteous sympathy and act like you care." Evelyn turned away to set the filled containers in a small cooler at her feet, but not before Agnes caught the sheen of tears glazing her eyes.

Oh, but she did know. In a way. Maybe not on the same level as Evelyn, but she remembered the ache in her chest, the sudden vacant feeling in her womb upon seeing the doctor's grim face.

"Losing someone you love creates an ache in your soul that's irreparable." Agnes softened her voice and reached for Evelyn's hand. "Forgiveness goes a long way in healing pain, Evelyn. This project can prevent other mothers from facing the same kind of grief you're dealing with."

Evelyn pulled her hand away and wiped it on her flowered skirt. "You're one to talk. Have you forgiven your ex-husband for all that he did to you?"

Agnes opened her mouth, but words escaped her as she stared at the woman's harsh expression.

"That's what I thought. So push your hypocritical soapbox out of my way so I can finish with these meals."

Ian threw his second horseshoe, then groaned when it landed with a thud in the dirt beside his first one instead of ringing the stake.

His head wasn't in the game.

Suggesting the race was meant to take Red's mind off Agape House since she'd been putting in a ton of hours lately. But once they reached the finish line, she bolted across the grass as if her hair were on fire. He hadn't seen her since.

How long did it take to grab a couple of drinks?

Maybe he needed to find her and make sure she was okay.

"Hey, guys, I'm out. Sorry. I need to go check on someone." He started across the field toward the pavilion but slowed as he spotted Mom folding her chair and moving away from her circle of friends.

Dad continued to play horseshoes without offering to carry her chair. And that fried Ian.

How could two people be at the same event yet each act as if the other one didn't exist?

Ian hadn't seen Dad in weeks, which was fine by him. Did he even know Chief Laughton had dropped by? Even at the office, Dad kept his door closed or worked from the cabin.

That should make Father's Day a real blast tomorrow.

Ian took the chair from Mom. "You okay?"

She brushed a strand of hair away from her face and smiled. "I'm fine, honey. Getting a little tired. I think I'm going to head home."

"You sure you don't need anything?"

"I'm sure."

"You talk to Dad?"

"No." She glanced at Dad laughing with the guys, then looked away, but not before Ian caught the sadness that flickered in her eyes.

"Why not?"

"He's bullheaded and won't listen to reason.

"You two can't let this come between you." Ian tightened his grip on the chair, hating this divide.

"And I can't let him keep our daughter from coming home either."

He placed a hand on her shoulder. "Don't worry, Mom. Zoe will be home. I promise."

"Sweetie, as much as I value your word, that's one thing you can't ensure."

"Okay, then. How about I'll do everything in my power to make sure Zoe comes home?"

Mom twisted her wedding band. "At what cost, though?"

"Dad'll come around. He's not going to throw away forty years of marriage over this."

A loud whoop caused Ian's head to turn toward the

horseshoe game. Dad thumped Max Peretti on the back, then turned and headed toward the pavilion.

"I'll be right back." He handed her the chair, then jogged across the grass to catch up with Dad.

"Dad."

Dad glanced over his shoulder but kept walking. "Ian."

Ian fell in step next to him. "You're acting like Mom's not even here."

"I tried to talk to her in the food line, but she walked away."

"You hurt her."

"I hurt her?" Dad stopped short and slammed him with a glare. He raked a hand through his hair, then turned away. "She went behind my back."

"No, Dad. She's been up-front about Agape House from day one, and you know it." Ian fisted his hands and pulled in a deep breath to calm the tension tightening his chest. "How can you be against something that will help people? Especially your own daughter?"

Dad tossed his hands in the air. "You and your mother have this idealized vision of Zoe coming home. Like we're going to be this happy family again. Ain't gonna happen. People like her don't change. I learned that lesson long ago."

Ian clenched his jaw as he struggled to keep his tone level. "Zoe's paying for her mistake."

"Mistake?" Dad's voice rose as he continued to gesture his hands. "She didn't run a red light, Ian. Her actions killed a guy."

Ian glanced around to see if they were drawing unnecessary attention, but everyone seemed preoccupied with their own activities. Still, it wouldn't hurt Dad to lower the volume.

"I'm well aware. I also know she regrets it more than anything. She learned her lesson."

"How do you know for sure?" Dad paused and scrubbed a hand over the back of his head. He looked off in the distance, his voice lowered. "I can't tell you the number of times I've heard, 'Daddy, I promise I won't drink ever again.'"

For a moment, Ian could imagine how painful that must have been on his parents—to have to deal with his sister's behavior time and time again.

"Zoe isn't sixteen anymore. She's spent the past four years of her life in prison for killing another person—her fiancé…her son's father. Don't you think that's going to change her? Where's your faith?"

What else did his sister have to do to prove her past was just that…in the past?

"I need more than faith, son. I've seen it happen way too many times. People promise they'll change—things will be different. But, over time, they fall back into their old ways. Then those who believed in them—encouraged them—are the ones ending up disappointed."

"You can't compare her to what your parents did to you." Ian kicked at the grass with the toe of his shoe. "I don't get it, Dad. You've always been there until…"

"Until?"

"Until Zoe went to prison. Then you just shut down, checked out. You turned your back on the rest of us."

"I've been there for you guys."

"Physically, maybe. But not emotionally. What happened with Zoe affected all of us. When I was growing up, you always told me family came first. You said you never wanted to be like your parents. You hated how they turned their backs on you. How is what you're doing any different?"

"Saw Harry Shaw a little bit ago. He said you rescheduled his appointment."

Harry Shaw? What did his client have to do with anything?

"I did."

"Why?"

"I ran out of time on Friday, so I rescheduled for Monday. He said he was fine with it. I'm seeing him first thing."

Dad crossed his arms over his chest. "Don't let this Agape business mess with your priorities."

Ian squared his shoulders and maintained eye contact. "Or what, Dad? You'll fire me?"

"Make sure your priorities are in order."

The words Ian wanted to spew at his dad blistered his tongue. The acid in his throat fed his anger. Chest heaving, Ian stood eye to eye with the one man he had looked up to all his life. "I could remind you of the same thing. You're either all in—make things work with Mom— or you're out for good, because you're destroying her one day at a time. Zoe nearly crushed her, but she has hope again. You won't take that away. Our family is my priority…something you seem to have forgotten."

Chapter Ten

Agnes couldn't stand it another minute longer.

The anguish in Ian's voice ripped through her soul, shredding her heart. Tears burned her eyes. She'd never heard him speak to Pete with such anger, but maybe it was the wake-up call his daddy needed to realign his priorities.

She walked behind Ian and placed her hands on his arms. His muscles quivered from the adrenaline surging through his veins. "Come on, Ian. Let's go."

Ian tore his gaze away from Pete's steely glare. Agnes gave Pete a sympathetic smile—her heart ached for him, too—but he turned on his heel and stalked toward the river that framed the south side of the park.

She wrapped her arm around Ian's waist and guided him to her convertible. He stumbled beside her without protest and crawled into the passenger side, slammed the door and rested his head against the back of the seat.

Agnes climbed behind the wheel, started the engine, then backed out of the parking lot.

Instead of heading toward town, she turned left and drove toward the lake sprawled against the horizon.

With the top down, her hair whipped around her face. Country music blared from the radio.

She drove along the stretch of highway around the lake. Canopies of evergreens shaded the afternoon sun, but allowed slashes of light to lattice the pavement.

"Pull over."

Spying a turnaround up ahead, Agnes edged the convertible off the side of the road and turned off the ignition.

They sat in silence except for the hypnotic lapping of the water against the shore and the wind ruffling the leaves overhead.

She undid her seat belt and opened the door. "Come on. Let's walk."

Ian followed, then waited as Agnes kicked off her platforms and tossed them in the backseat.

Going barefoot was better than breaking an ankle as they cut through the trees and scrambled down the dirt path that lead to the gravel shore.

Sun-drenched rocks stabbed the bottoms of her feet. She rolled up her pant legs, then waded ankle deep in the water, sucking in a sudden breath as the icy water lapped over her toes.

Ian kicked off his loafers, emptied his pockets, dropping his phone, keys and wallet inside his shoes. He yanked off his T-shirt and pitched it to the ground.

Without a word, he tore into the water until he was waist deep, then disappeared beneath the surface.

A moment later, he smashed through the glassy facade and gasped for breath.

He swam, his strong arms pushing him forward with even strokes, until he was a quarter-sized spot in the water.

Agnes stepped out of the water and sat on the bank next to his things with her knees tucked beneath her chin.

Ian treaded water for a few minutes, then turned and swam back to shore. Once he reached the shore, he stood and shook his head before plodding back to her.

He yanked his shirt over his head and nodded to a nearby boulder. "Let's sit on that rock so I can dry out before getting back into your car."

Barefoot, he scaled the rock, then reached down to help her up.

Chest heaving and breathing ragged, Ian sat on the edge, clasped his arms around his legs and rested his forehead on his knees.

She settled beside him, tucking her feet under her thighs, and rested a hand on his shoulder. Just to let him know she was here for him.

A shudder coursed through him. He ran a finger and thumb over his eyes. Agnes couldn't be sure if the wetness was only lake water.

Ian reached for her hand and squeezed but didn't release it. "Thanks."

"You're welcome."

"I'm sorry if I embarrassed you."

She laughed. "Ian, we've been friends for far too long for you to worry about that now." She fought the urge to comb his hair away from his face.

Ian covered his face with his hands, then exhaled loudly. "I shouldn't have flown off the handle like that, but Dad's being such a jerk. I can't stand the way he's treating Mom."

"He's hurting."

He glanced at her with an *Are you kidding me?* look plastered on his face. "We're all hurting, Red. But that doesn't mean we walk out on family."

"Your dad will come around, Ian. He has his own issues to deal with. Try to be more understanding."

"He drives me nuts at times. He's so black-and-white."

"Yeah, but he's still your dad. You need to show him respect."

"Respect is earned. And right now he's losing mine."

"Don't be that way. Your family is going through enough already. Grace goes a long way to mending fences."

He stared at the lake. "Yeah, I guess."

"You guess? Imagine if that's how God dealt with us…there goes that crazy redhead screwing up again… I guess I'll show her some grace."

"God loves you, Red." He wrapped an arm around her and folded her into his embrace.

She pressed her cheek against his damp chest. "Yeah, I know."

The serenity of the lake flowed over her. She breathed in the pine-scented air, and for the first time all day, she relaxed.

Even though Ian remained as knotted as a sailor's rope, peace filtered through every pore of her body. For the moment with only nature as a choir, she knew everything was going to work out.

Pete and Charlotte would make up. The Agape team would make their deadline. Zoe would be home.

Ian removed his arm and reached for her hand. He ran his thumb over her knuckles. "You have remarkable hands. Long elegant fingers."

What was he doing? His touch was so gentle, intimate—something one said to someone…loved.

Turning to face her, he slid his fingers through her hair, combing it away from her cheek. His eyes darkened. The pad of his thumb caressed the curve of her ear, and then he trailed his fingers down the hollow of her neck, following the contours of her jaw.

Her breath caught as his gentle touch explored her face. She closed her eyes, not thinking, just feeling as his index finger outlined her lips.

She swallowed, hating to break the spell. "Ian?" The hoarseness of her voice sounded dry, like gravel rubbing together.

"Shh." He rested a finger against her lips.

She opened her eyes to find him inches from her face. Her gaze tangled with his as he moved closer.

Her heart crashed against her rib cage like a stormy wave, capturing her breath and threatening to pull her into the undertow.

When she couldn't last another breath, his lips touched hers, kissing her with a sweet gentleness that resurrected her soul.

She wrapped her arms around his neck, threading her fingers through his damp hair.

He tangled his fingers in her curls as he pulled her closer and deepened the kiss.

Ian dragged his lips from her mouth and buried his face in her neck. His ragged breathing warmed her collarbone.

She kept a hand around his neck and rested her cheek against his wet head.

The reality of the situation washed over her.

She shifted, pulling away slightly, immediately missing his closeness.

Ian looked up and swiped a lock of hair off her forehead.

"You are so beautiful." His whispered words seeped into the cracks and crevices of her heart. Piece by piece, she began to feel whole again.

She touched her lips where the warmth of his mouth still lingered, then looked down at his other hand resting on her knee. She stroked his muscled forearm with her fingernails.

"Ian? What just happened?"

Ian turned his hand and captured hers, entwining their fingers. "I kissed you. Apparently not well enough if you're unsure. But I do seem to recall you kissing me back."

Yes, she did.

She couldn't hold back a smile. The kiss was…wow… who knew? Yes, most definitely a nice kiss.

She glanced at him through her lashes, feeling a little uncertain. "I mean why?"

"Would you believe me if I said I've been wanting to do it for years?"

"But that's crazy. We're friends."

"You're my best friend, Red. But you're so much more than that." He kind of chuckled, but she couldn't find the humor in his words. "The thing is…" He pulled air into his lungs, then released it slowly. Then he grabbed both hands and squeezed. "The thing is I've been in love with you for years."

Her heart should have been exploding with joy. Hadn't she longed to hear him say those words? So why wasn't she repeating the same words that were teetering on the tip of her tongue?

"But you can't love me." She pulled her gaze away from his and stared at the expanse of the lake stretching in front of them.

"Why not?"

"Because I'm…I'm broken. You deserve to be with someone who can give you want you truly need."

"No, Red." He caught one of her curls and twirled it

around his finger. "I need you. Only you. It's always been you. You're perfect just the way you are."

Tears filled her eyes. A sob rose in her chest. "Oh, Ian. I'm not. I..."

She wanted to tell him. To bare her soul—her darkest secret, but she couldn't face him walking away. Not just yet.

He rested his forehead against hers. "You're perfect for me. And that's what matters."

But that wasn't all that mattered.

Ian wanted a family—deserved a family. And she couldn't be the one to give it to him.

And what about their friendship? What about when Ian decided what she had to offer wasn't enough? What about when he tossed her aside after determining she had no real value?

What then?

No, all that mattered was she couldn't fall in love with her best friend. Because if she admitted how she felt about him, and he didn't want her anymore, then she'd lose everything. And she was quite sure her heart would be beyond restoration.

He wanted to spend the day at the cabin with his dad about as much as he wanted to drive to the prison almost every weekend. But duty called.

And after talking to Red yesterday, he needed to do a better job of showing grace.

Ian grabbed the gift bag and opened his door. "Come on, Bubba. Let's go wish Grandpa a happy Father's Day."

So maybe he had said some things that needed to be said, but yesterday's church picnic wasn't the time or the place for a confrontation.

Griffin charged up the wide porch steps of the cabin

and flung open the screen door. "Happy Father's Day, Grandpa."

Ian caught it before it slammed and trudged inside. Oldies music blasted from the radio on the windowsill. The scent of turpentine lingered in the air, coating his throat.

Ian dropped the bag on the table and headed for the kitchen sink. He grabbed a plastic cup out of the dish drainer and filled it with cold water. Drinking it washed the nasty taste out of his mouth and gave him a moment to figure out what to say. He drained the glass and set it in the dishpan.

He walked back into the living room and found Dad at his easel. Griffin wasn't with him. Maybe he had gone up to the loft bedroom for something.

Dad reached over and turned down the volume, then nodded at Ian.

He took in the dark circles under Dad's eyes and the lines etching his forehead. So he wasn't the only one who didn't sleep last night.

Between stressing about Dad and replaying that kiss with Red...he had spent most of the night staring at his ceiling.

"Happy Father's Day." Ian handed him the gift bag.

"Thanks, son." He looked inside and pulled out a black case. He opened it and ran a finger over the red sable brushes. Smiling, he closed the case. "These are great, thanks."

"Wanna grab a bite to eat or something?" Maybe getting out of the cabin would help him feel less crowded in by the elephant in the room.

"Yeah, sure. Sounds good. Let me clean up this mess first and change my clothes. Where are you thinking?"

Ian shrugged. "It's your day. You pick it."

Dad carried his palette and brushes to the sink. "What's your mother doing today?"

Ian sat on the couch, picked up yesterday's paper and scanned the headlines. "When we left, she was reading."

"How about if I give her a call and see if she wants to join us?" Dad's voice sounded hesitant.

Ian read the same headline about the school district budget cuts three times before he responded, "I think she'd like that."

Dad returned to the living room, grabbed his cell phone and headed out to the front porch, the screen door slamming behind him.

Griffin returned to the living room wearing blue swim trunks and carrying a red and white towel over his shoulder.

"Where are you going, Bubba?"

"I wanna go swimming. I'm so hot and sweaty."

"You know you can't go to the lake by yourself."

"I know. I was hoping you'd take me."

"We're taking Grandpa out to dinner."

"Just a quick dip to cool off? Then I promise to get ready superfast to go to dinner."

"Fine by me, but double-check with Grandpa. He's on the porch talking to Gram on the phone." Ian tossed the paper on the coffee table and stood.

Through the window, Ian watched as Griffin waited for a turn to talk. Ian couldn't make out what they were saying, but Griffin's fist pump in the air let him know Dad said yes.

Griffin pressed his face into the screen. "Grandpa said I could go swimming since we're not going anywhere. Grandma's coming here."

Just like old times.

Since Zoe left, they hadn't done any of the usual family traditions.

"Let's get some sunblock on you, Bubba, or Gram will ground me for letting you burn." Ian grabbed a bottle of sunblock Mom kept in a bucket by the front door and shook it.

Griffin squirmed while Ian smeared the lotion on him.

Since Dad was still on the phone, Ian gestured toward the lake to let him know where they were going.

Dad nodded and gave him a thumbs-up.

They headed down the steps. Ian carried Griffin's towel while the kid ran down the rutted path through the hedge of trees that parted to reveal greenish-blue water dappled with liquid silver.

Griffin plowed into the water without hesitation or fear. A kid after his own heart. Growing up on the water, they learned young how to swim. Griffin surfaced, then fell back and backstroked.

Gray plumes of campfire smoke billowed over the treetops and smudged the blue sky. The scent of grilling meat wafted through the air, causing Ian's stomach to grumble. Along the horizon, canoers glided through the water.

Ian kicked off his deck shoes and sat on the sand. Pulling his knees to his chest, he wrapped his arms around his legs and scanned the shore across the lake to find the rock he had shared with Agnes yesterday.

His new favorite spot.

Kissing her was even better than he'd imagined. Her soft lips, silky skin. And he wanted to do it again. For the rest of his life. But he sensed her retreat. He needed to take it slow.

They had sat on the rock for a while, talking about Ian's outburst with Dad and how he could have handled it better. At least Agnes didn't scold him like a child. She sympathized with him but let him know there was enough strife in the family without adding it.

And she was right.

He needed to apologize to Dad.

As if the guy could read his thoughts, Ian sensed someone behind him. Dad walked barefoot across the sand and sat beside Ian.

Griffin waved and then dove under the water.

"The kid's a fish." Maybe small talk would break the ice.

Dad kept his eyes on the water. "Just like you were at that age."

Ian grabbed a handful of sand and sifted it through his fingers. "Listen, Dad…about yesterday. I'm sorry."

Dad rested his elbows on his bent knees. "Me, too, son. Me, too. But you were right. I turned my back on you guys. The past few years haven't been easy on any of us."

"No, but we've been handling it."

"Yeah, but I should've stepped up and done a better job. You've put your life on hold to help out with Griffin. That's not fair to you."

"My life is fine."

His heart ached to spend his life with Red.

"I talked with your mother. She's pulling steaks out of the freezer. We're going to hang out here and grill if that's okay with you."

"Sounds great."

"Tomorrow I'm going through Agape House with your mother. Then you and I can sit down and talk about the best way for me to help you."

"You serious?"

"Yes, it's time I manned up and took care of my family."

Ian was thankful for his sunglasses so his dad wouldn't see his eyes filling with tears.

"What's Agnes doing today? Give her a call and see if she wants to join us. Father's Day must be tough since Chuck passed."

"I can, but I suspect she'll say she's busy."

"You two have a fight?"

"Not at all. Quite the opposite, in fact." Ian told Dad about the drive to the rock and the kiss.

"It's about time, son. You've been pining for that girl since you were fifteen."

"I feel like she's pushing me away…keeping me at arm's length."

Dad slapped him on the back. "Don't lose hope. You've waited this long. She'll come around."

Hope.

That elusive word spurred his courage to push their relationship a bit further, to encourage her to step outside her comfort zone in order to give them a chance at a future together.

Despite the kiss and the way their relationship continued to evolve, he couldn't help wondering if it was temporary. For him, though, there was no going back to the way things used to be. Could he live with that if she rejected him?

Chapter Eleven

A gnes was going to be late for work if she didn't step on it. She smothered a yawn, grabbed her keys and slid the purse strap onto her shoulder before letting herself out the side door and locking it behind her.

She opened the car door and started to slide in, but a handpicked bouquet of white daisies, yellow buttercups, purple sweet peas and Queen Anne's lace wrapped in a damp paper towel lay on the seat.

A note fluttered down and landed on the floorboard. She reached for it and recognized Ian's scrawl:

Saw these on my way to work and thought of you.

When was the last time anyone had given her flowers? The simple gesture warmed her heart.

She hadn't seen Ian since Saturday when he kissed her on the rock and declared his love. Even though she needed a little space to process everything, that didn't keep her from reliving their kiss.

Smiling, she buried her nose in the petals, which caused her to sneeze repeatedly.

Okay, so that was a stupid thing to do.

She set the flowers on the passenger seat and slid behind the wheel. She'd have to put them in water at the coffee shop, not having time to head back inside the house.

Five minutes later, she crossed the bridge over the Shelby River and headed toward Cuppa Josie's but then noticed the thermostat on her dash heading toward the hot zone.

Odd.

She could understand the July heat having something to do with it, but her car hadn't been running that long.

For the past week, it had been in the low nineties before noon. She felt as if she were back in Texas again. If the gathering storm clouds were anything to go by, rain would soon bring relief from the sticky heat.

To be safe, though, she'd call Buck's Garage and set up an appointment to get her car serviced.

A quick glance in her rearview mirror showed a trail of smoke, at about the same time the smell of burning liquid seeped into the car.

She gripped the steering wheel. "No. No. No. No."

This couldn't be happening.

She had spent enough time hanging out in the garage talking to Daddy when he worked on the convertible to know that smell was antifreeze…and her savings account would soon be incinerated.

She signaled to pull off to the side of the road, but before she could edge over completely, the power shut down. She shifted into Neutral and coasted to the curb as she muscled the steering wheel to park in a somewhat parallel position.

Steam billowed out from under her hood.

She pounded her palm against the steering wheel.

This was not going to be a cheap fix.

Now, what was she going to do?

Getting to work wasn't a problem—she could walk

the couple of blocks, but Buck's Garage was on the other side of town.

Maybe she could call him from Cuppa Josie's and have him tow her car to the garage.

Another bill she wasn't looking forward to, but what choice did she have?

But first, she needed to give Josie a call and let her know she was going to be a few minutes late.

Dragging her purse into her lap, she rummaged through the mess for her phone but couldn't find it.

Mama had called while she was putting on her makeup. Her phone was probably still sitting by the bathroom sink.

Well, didn't that just beat all!

No use sitting here and moaning about something she couldn't fix. She yanked her keys from the ignition, grabbed her purse and Ian's bouquet of flowers, then scooted out of the car, locking it behind her.

Halfway down the second block, she felt like a wilted daisy. Sweat dribbled from her hairline to her shoulder blades.

A loud crack like a tree splitting caused her to jump. The sky unleashed its fury.

Rain plastered her uniform to her skin and soaked her hair.

She sprinted down the sidewalk, shot through the alley behind Cuppa Josie's and wrenched open the back door.

Seeing the kitchen lights on and hearing Josie's iPod playing, Agnes dripped water across the floor as she hurried to the storeroom in search of a towel. "Sorry, I'm late. My car died just past the bridge. Then it poured half a block away."

Josie sat at the kitchen counter drizzling icing over warm cinnamon rolls. The scent of sugar and cinnamon mingled with brewing coffee. "No worries. Don't forget I have a doctor's appointment in a little bit."

"Give me a few minutes to dry off, and I'll be as right as rain." Okay, bad choice of words at the moment.

Agnes dropped her purse and the crushed bouquet of flowers on the corner of the counter. She grabbed her emergency bag out of Josie's office, then headed to the bathroom to change and fix her hair. After touching up her makeup and refastening her still-damp ponytail, she returned to the kitchen and tied an apron around her waist. She filled a canning jar with water for the flowers, but when she picked them up, they drooped in her hand.

"Pretty posies."

"Thanks. I found them on my car seat this morning. They're a bit crushed from the rain."

"Put them in water anyway. Maybe they'll perk up."

She did, but before Josie could ask more questions about where the flowers came from, Agnes headed for the dining room. She flicked on the lights and unlocked the front door after turning the closed sign to Open.

A glance at the pastry case showed Josie had already filled it, which pushed Agnes's guilt meter up another notch. She headed for the kitchen to grab the air pots of coffee.

She expected a steady stream of customers driven inside by the rain.

Once the coffee bar had been set up, she paused a moment to pour hot water over a French vanilla tea bag and let it seep for a minute.

The front door opened, and Ian stepped inside. He half closed his umbrella and leaned it against the rack behind the door. Rain dotted his blue heather V-neck T-shirt, turning it almost black in spots. He wore tan cargo pants and brown leather work boots.

The sight of him curled her stomach and sent a shot of anticipation through her system.

Since no one else was in the dining room, Agnes rounded the counter and met him halfway, standing close enough to breath in his freshly showered scent. "Good morning."

With her insides trembling and showing more bravery than she actually felt, she placed a hand on his chest and brushed a kiss across his lips. "Thanks for the flowers."

"If that's what it takes for a kiss, I'll give you flowers hourly." A grin spread slowly across his face as his eyes darkened. He pulled her close and gave her another kiss—a longer, more welcoming one. "Now, this is what I call service. I hope you don't greet all your customers this way."

"Only the really special ones." She pressed a cheek to his chest and listened to his heartbeat.

"Hopefully I don't have much competition."

She sighed, then stepped back, considering Josie didn't pay her to hug on her friend during working hours. "Not much. What brings you by so early?"

"I'm concerned about a tree behind Agape House, but I need the rain to let up before I can check it out. Since I was up anyway, I decided to grab coffee. I'm going to the office for a bit until the storm clears out."

"Smart choice. Josie made fresh cinnamon rolls this morning. Want one to go with your coffee?"

"Are you able to join me?"

Agnes glanced around the empty dining room and smirked. "Looks like everyone can fend for themselves for a minute or two."

"What happened to your car? I saw it sitting on the other side of the bridge."

"Thanks for the reminder. I need to call Buck." She told him about the car trouble she had.

He whistled low and through his teeth. "Ouch, Red. That's going to be expensive."

"Please don't remind me. I'm just sick about it."

"I can help you out, you know."

"Thanks, but I'll handle it."

"Listen, Red—"

She put up a hand. "I got it covered…don't worry."

"Well, the offer's still there."

"I know. I appreciate it, but I'll take care of it."

"How about dinner tonight? Maybe around six?"

"Sure, sounds great. Have a seat, and I'll bring your cinnamon roll right out."

Agnes pushed through the swinging door into the kitchen and reached for a spatula to remove two cinnamon rolls from the pan.

"Did my eyes deceive me, or did I just see you locking lips with Ian James?" Josie asked.

Heat spread up Agnes's neck faster than melted icing over warm rolls. "Um…"

"Agnes, just what have you been keeping from me?"

"Can we talk about this later?" She didn't want to get into it with her friend, especially when she was still trying to untangle her own mixed emotions.

"Only if you promise to spill every delicious detail."

"Promise." Agnes crooked her pinkie in Josie's direction."

Josie cinched hers around Agnes's and squeezed. "That man has been after you for years. So glad you finally had the good sense to see what was right in front of you."

Agnes didn't reply as she slid the cinnamon rolls onto two plates and licked leftover icing off her thumb.

She couldn't explain why she kissed Ian a few minutes ago, or even allowed him to kiss her back. She simply wanted to enjoy the moment without thinking about the consequences.

She carried the cinnamon rolls to the dining room and sat them on the two-seater Ian sat at reading the morning paper.

"How was Father's Day with your dad?"

"Good. We talked things out and realized we had both made mistakes. Dad's going to try harder with Agape House, and I'm going to back off. Mom came out, and we grilled steaks while Griffin swam. You should have joined us."

Agnes placed a hand on his shoulder. "I'm so glad, Ian. And you and your family didn't need me hanging around while you made your peace. Be right back, I need to call Buck."

She ducked behind the counter and pulled the phone book from the door under the register. After finding Buck's number, she dialed and waited for him to pick up. Once he answered, she explained the problem. He rambled for a few minutes, then quoted her an estimated price to fix her car. The number was a sucker punch to her gut...the cost wiping out most of her savings. Her down payment for the cottage.

Resting her elbow on the counter, she rubbed her forehead. Any practical person would tell her to ditch the relic and buy something more economical, but the convertible had been her daddy's, passed on to her after graduation. Giving it up was losing her last link to him.

But the cottage was the kind of home she always wanted to have.

She couldn't mention anything to Ian about it...

he'd offer to pay for it or loan her the cash, which she
didn't want.

This was her problem and she'd find the solution, but
no matter what she chose, she'd have to make a sacrifice
that snagged a piece of her heart.

Could life get any better?

Maybe his concerns about Red were his own paranoia.
Her greeting at the coffee shop was anything but keeping him at arm's length. He'd still have to tread lightly
not to spook her.

Whistling, he jogged through the rain and opened the
door to James & Son Insurance. He dropped his umbrella
in the stand next to the door and sauntered past the cocoa-
colored leather sofa in the reception area and nodded to
Jess, the receptionist he shared with Dad.

In his office, he pulled back the heavy burgundy floor-
to-ceiling drapes to allow light to spill across the polished floor.

Sitting in his executive chair behind his wooden desk,
he laced his fingers behind his head and swiveled the
chair to watch the rain bullet the Shelby River.

His eyes skimmed over his college diploma hanging
on the wall next to the window and settled on one of his
favorite photos—he and Red holding the Golden Paddle
Award they had won during the canoe races that year.

The same year Bobby Levine decided he was interested in her and did his best to win Red's attention. The
guy was too much of an idiot to hold on to a good thing
when he had it.

But seeing the rowboat sparked an idea.

Ian swiveled around to his desk and opened his laptop. He typed in the URL for the local weather. The rain
was projected to stop by evening.

Maybe instead of dinner, she'd be willing to have a picnic and take the boat out before dark. He pulled out his cell phone and tapped out a text to ask her.

Dad poked his head into Ian's office. "Got a minute, son?"

He hit Send. "Sure, Dad. What's up?"

"You're not busy?" He pointed to Ian's phone in his hand.

"No, I was texting Red about possible dinner plans tonight."

Dad dropped in one of the chairs in front of Ian's desk and leaned forward and clasped his hands. "Patrick Laughton just left."

"Again? Griffin wrote his sister a note of apology, and I sent a check to cover the damage to her yard ornament. We've made sure to stay out of her way."

Dad held up a hand. "I know."

"Then what's the problem?" Ian laced his hands behind his head and leaned back in his chair.

"Apparently she had words with Agnes." Dad stood and shoved his hands in his pockets. He paced in front of Ian's desk.

Ian sat forward. "Red? When?"

"I guess it was at the church picnic."

That explained Red's absence when she disappeared to get the two of them a cold drink.

But why didn't she say something about it?

"So what happened?" Ian dragged a hand through his hair.

"Apparently Iris told him about their sister's heated discussion with Agnes and learned Evelyn mailed a letter to the parole board to block Zoe's release. Then she mailed a letter to the city council, requesting closure of Agape House."

Ian exhaled into his hands. The coffee he just drank burned his stomach.

"Dad, Zoe had nothing to do with Evelyn's son's death. She was only nine or ten when he was killed."

"I know that, but she sees women like Zoe getting a second chance when her son doesn't."

"I feel bad for her, Dad." Ian pushed back his chair and stood. He rounded his desk and matched Dad's strides. "No parent should ever have to lose a kid like that."

"There's something else to consider, too. When Zoe had the accident and Kyle Jacoby was killed, his parents wanted nothing to do with Griffin. Patrick said they've been notified of Zoe's pending release, and they're not happy. We have to be prepared for their possible petition to keep her behind bars."

"Can they do that?" Ian leaned against his desk and dropped his head to his chest. A dull ache formed at the back of his skull.

Dad sighed and nodded. "Yes, apparently anyone can speak out against Zoe being released."

"So what now?"

"Keep praying. Last night your mother mentioned she goes there every morning and prays through each room, then walks around the block and asks for God's protection for the women coming in and for their families. Her faith is strong, and she believes in this project. I told her I'd do whatever I can to make sure this project succeeds."

Hearing his Dad's changed attitude refreshed him, but Ian couldn't help wondering at his change of heart. "What convinced you in the end, Dad?"

"I love your mother. And I love being married to her. Forty years ago I made a promise, which she reminded me of." Dad sighed and leaned against the desk. "The night before our wedding, she called and offered me one last chance to back out. She said once we exchanged vows, she was holding me to them because divorce wasn't an option. She refused to put you kids through what she went through as a child when her parents separated."

"She's a smart woman."

"She's the best. And I was an idiot to turn my back on her the way I did. But we're working through it. Speaking of smart women, what's going on with you and Agnes Joy?"

"I'm still not sure how she feels, but I can tell her walls are crumbling."

"If you don't mind your old man's advice—take it slow. Give her time to get used to the new changes in your relationship. Show her she's worth waiting for."

As predicted, the rain stopped and the clouds cleared away, taking the oppressing humidity with it. The evening sun stretched across the lake.

Ian released the rope and pulled the aluminum rowboat to the end of the dock so he and Red could get in for their dinner date.

Reaching for Red's hand, he helped her into the boat. She settled on one of the benches and snapped a faded life jacket over her white T-shirt. She leaned back, closed her eyes and sighed as the breeze played with her hair.

"Long day?"

"Yes, the rain brought people inside all afternoon. I'm glad it cleared out for a bit this evening."

"Me, too."

Taking his place in the middle of the boat and facing the stern, he leaned forward, then pulled back to paddle the boat away from the dock.

The oarlocks squeaked as he rowed past the marshy bank where bullfrogs croaked. Gulls cawed and circled overhead. A pair of dragonflies darted between them and danced on the surface of the water.

A peace he hadn't felt in a long time rippled through him. Even with the challenges they continued to face with Agape House and trying to get Zoe released, he knew things would work out. God had a plan.

Agnes sat up and rubbed her stomach. "What time's dinner?"

He lifted the oars up and set them just inside the boat. Then he reached under his seat for a soft-sided cooler, unzipped it and pulled out a couple of sandwiches and two cans of Coke, handing her one of each. He pulled out a wicker basket and opened it, displaying several small bags of chips and a container filled with Mom's chocolate chip cookies.

She set the soda next to her, then unwrapped a turkey and cheese on whole wheat and took a bite. "Thank you."

"Nothing fancy."

"It's perfect." She shivered as a small gust of wind blew over them. Goose bumps pebbled her skin.

He reached under her bench and pulled out a rolled blanket. He shook out the navy fleece and tucked it around her legs. "How's that?"

"You always think of everything."

"I try."

She looked off in the distance as she finished her sandwich. "Ian, I have to be honest and tell you I'm scared."

"About what?"

"About you. Us. Messing this up."

At least she was willing to acknowledge the changes in their relationship. That gave him hope.

He twirled one of her crazy curls around his finger. "Sweetheart, you can't mess this up. We have the rest of our lives to figure things out."

"Is that a proposal?" She shot him a sidelong glance through her fringed lashes, but her question stopped his heart from beating momentarily.

He struggled to find the right words. Again, he wanted to be careful not to rush things. "Do you want it to be?"

Instead of saying anything, she popped the tab on her can and sipped her Coke.

Okay, so maybe that wasn't the response he wanted, but he'd give it time.

"Relax, I'm not going to push you. I've waited this long."

She trailed her fingers in the water. "What do we tell people?"

"About what?"

"Us."

"Tell them what you want. Listen, Red, I know you had a long day, and you'll be ready to crash soon, but don't overthink this. Just let it progress naturally." He leaned forward and rested his hands on her knees.

"Thank you. Just don't freak out when I get a little crazy every now and then."

"I've been dealing with your crazy for years."

She threaded her fingers through his. "Do you remember my senior prom?"

He smiled and gave her hands a gentle squeeze. "Of course. How could I forget? Matt Wilson's case of strep throat was my gain."

"You were so sweet for stepping in at the last minute to be my date."

"I enjoyed every minute of it. What made you think of that now anyway?"

She shrugged. "I don't know. I was thinking about the first time you kissed me."

"My favorite part of the night. And right after you told me you liked me."

"Yeah, I was crazy for doing that. It made things weird between us." She pulled her hands away and reached for her Coke.

Overhead, a flock of geese honked as they flew past.

Ian rested his elbows on his knees and clasped his hands. "You weren't crazy, Red. I was the crazy one for not doing anything about it."

"I was so sure you felt the same way. Otherwise I would have kept my mouth shut."

"I did feel the same way. But I thought I needed to let you go experience life beyond the lake. I didn't want you to feel tied down in a long distance relationship."

"So you've said several times." She dragged a hand through her hair. "We could have made it work. As much as I loved Texas, it wasn't the same as when I was a child. I missed the lake. I missed you."

"Seemed like you missed Bobby more."

She snorted. "Hardly. When I came home at Christmas, you said you had met someone, remember? You told me we had a great night, but you couldn't let that stand in the way of my future."

"Had I known you would have gone running to him... Like I said, I was an idiot."

"Yeah, too bad life doesn't come with do-overs."

"We can't go back, Red. Only forward. And you're the only one I want in my future."

"You're wonderful, Ian. Just let me get a little used to the idea of us before we rush into something more."

"We'll take all the time you need. Like I said, I'm not going anywhere." He leaned forward, laced his fingers with hers and brushed a gentle kiss across her lips, savoring the sweetness she offered.

"Let's focus on Zoe coming home before we make any long-term plans. Both of our plates are full enough right now."

"Fair enough."

She pulled away and touched her forehead to his. "I'm so glad you asked me to dinner, and I love the boat ride, but I'm so tired that I could curl up in a ball and sleep on the floor of this boat."

Ian laughed and reached for the oars. "Let's get you home, Sleeping Beauty."

Hopefully soon, he wouldn't have to drop her off at home and head back to his place. He was looking forward to the day when they could go to their home together. Someday.

Chapter Twelve

Darting a quick look at the darkening sky, Ian tugged off his ball cap and wiped away the sweat from his brow with his forearm. He needed to finish this roof before the brewing storm hit.

Crazy July weather. Storms one day, sun the next, then more storms.

He reached for his bottle of water and chugged the rest, grateful for the liquid in his parched throat even if it was as warm as a mud puddle. He poured the last few drops over his soaked head.

His back and shoulders ached from being hunched over for the past couple of hours, but the roof needed to be finished. He hadn't spent nearly as much time on it as he should have.

All he wanted to do was be with Red.

She quenched a thirst that had welled up inside him for so long. Her ability to make him laugh, her incredible beauty and the easy way she slid into his arms…things were almost perfect.

A ring on her finger would make it complete.

All in due time.

Hearing car doors closing behind him, he looked

over his shoulder to see Mom and Dad heading for the front door.

He gathered his tools, climbed down the ladder and dropped them in the back of his SUV. He snagged a fresh bottle of water from the cooler, then headed for the house.

The darkened rooms offered respite from the oppressive humidity outside.

"Hey. What's up?" Ian twisted the cap off his fresh bottle of water and guzzled half of it. He wiped the back of his hand across his mouth, then frowned.

Why weren't they saying anything?

Mom and Dad exchanged "that look"—the one he saw growing up that preceded bad news. His stomach tightened.

"What's going on? What happened?"

Blinking back tears, Mom gripped her purse strap and shifted her gaze to Dad. She gave him a slight nod.

Dad ran a hand over his head. "Wally Banks decided to pull his funding."

Ian stared at them as Dad's words sank in. "What? Why? Without his contributions, we won't be able to finish. He's our largest supporter."

Dad pressed his back against the wall and crossed his feet at the ankles. "Being on the city council, he learned about Evelyn Parnell's letter about Agape House and decided maybe she's right."

"That's it? No other reasoning? Well, that's just beautiful."

Mom sat on the bottom step of the staircase and looked up at him. "Have you asked Agnes about her conversation with Evelyn?"

Ian rested an elbow on the mantel. "No, it hasn't come up."

"What hasn't come up?" The three of them turned to

find Red coming into the living room from the kitchen, peeling purple gardening gloves off her hands. She wore cutoffs and a cute little pink T-shirt smudged with dirt. Her hair had been caught up in a ponytail, but pieces drifted around her ears and chin.

With his parents' surprise appearance, he had forgotten she was working in the backyard, weeding the flower beds and pruning the hedges. If his parents weren't there, he would have crossed the room and kissed her.

She stood on tiptoe and kissed Dad on the cheek, then turned to give Mom a hug. "All y'all's faces look downer than a hound's at the end of racoon season. What's going on?"

"We have a small problem." Ian tucked a piece of hair behind her ear and wiped a smudge of dirt off her nose.

"What kind of problem?"

"Evelyn Parnell sent a letter to the parole board, trying to block Zoe's release." Mom's voice sounded tiny in the hollow room.

Red wrapped an arm around Mom's shoulders. "Why?"

Ian pushed away from the mantel and started pacing. "That's not all. She sent a similar letter to the Shelby Lake City Council trying to keep Agape House from opening."

"Well, it's no secret she's against this place." She turned to Mom. "But you've done everything by the book."

Mom nodded, but her eyes dimmed. "I made sure I dotted every *I* and crossed every *T* so when something like this happened, I couldn't be held accountable."

"Did something else happen?" Red looked between the three of them.

"Yes, Wally Banks pulled his funding." Fatigue threaded Dad's words.

They were all getting tired of the setbacks.

Red glanced at him. "Wally Banks from the city council?"

He nodded. "Yes, apparently he read Evelyn's letter and decided to side with her. If he can get the other council members to back Evelyn, then Agape House is done."

Red jumped her feet and balled her hands into fists. "Zoe needs this place."

Ian scrubbed a hand over his face. "Preaching to the choir, babe."

"So what can we do?"

"Do? Don't you think you've done enough?" Now, why did he say something stupid like that?

Her eyes narrowed. "What are you talking about?"

"Chief Laughton paid Dad another visit. Something about your conversation with Evelyn?"

Red bristled and crossed her arms over her chest. "Oh, so this is my fault?"

Mom rose and glared at him before giving Red a one-armed hug. "No one is blaming you."

Somehow he needed to pry his foot from his mouth. Judging by the thunderous look on Red's face, this was going to take more than sweet-talking. Problem was, he wasn't feeling too sweet at the moment.

"Mom's right. Evelyn made her own decision, but just what did you say to her?"

"The woman was being ugly, and I defended y'all. She spewed poison faster than a rattlesnake in a bear trap. I told her everyone deserved a second chance and suggested forgiveness might go a long way in helping her heal. I promise y'all I didn't return the ugly one bit."

"But why did you have to say anything at all? Why couldn't you have ignored her?"

"But the things she was saying, Ian—"

"I don't care about her petty gossip. Neither should you. I thought your skin was tougher than that."

"My skin's just fine, thank you very much. But I couldn't stand by and listen to her bash my closest friends."

"You need to apologize to her and smooth things over."

"No." She crossed her arms over her chest and jutted her chin.

"Excuse me?"

"There's nothing wrong with your hearing, Ian."

"Do you realize what you've done?"

"Yes, I've stood up for your family. And I'll do it again. I refuse to let that woman torment your family. Your mama has worked her tail off to get this project off the ground. If you lose support, then you didn't need those donors in the first place. God will provide the necessary funds for Agape House."

"So mighty and righteous of you to say that from the cheap seats. You're not invested in this like I am."

"No, I don't obsess over every detail like you. Or fly off the handle over some biddy's idle threat. But don't say I'm not invested. Because if you believe that, then you're a fool."

One step forward. Two steps back.

Was that how her relationship was going to be with Ian?

If this impromptu silent auction at Cuppa Josie's to benefit Agape House went off without a hitch, then maybe they could make amends.

She hated the awkwardness between them over the past few days. How did things spiral out of control so quickly?

Agnes ran her hand over the curved drawers of the aqua-colored restored nightstand she'd bought at the thrift

store for a couple of bucks. The piece needed some attention and TLC to restore its purpose. Same with the stenciled dresser, a couple of club chairs, a piecrust table she
rescued from next to a Dumpster. Someone else's trash
became her treasure.

"The auction will be great." Josie stood behind Agnes
in the side dining room and placed her hands on her
shoulders. "Stop worrying."

Agnes moved a carved half-moon table against the
wall under the front window. "Thanks again for letting
me have the auction at the coffee shop, Sugar Pie."

"No problem. I love the pieces you brought. But make
sure you're doing this for the right reasons." She fluffed
a red-and-yellow-patterned pillow and returned it to the
twin bed frame Agnes had turned into a bench. "People can browse in this room. You've given them a lot of
choices."

When Agnes first came up with the idea of auction-
ing off some of her restored pieces, Josie had offered her
the side dining room at the coffee shop. Nick had cleared
out the tables, which gave plenty of space to arrange the
furniture, giving prospective buyers room to browse.

"If I sell everything I brought in, it'll just be a drop
in a bucket compared to what Wally was donating, but I
want to help Charlotte recoup a little of what she's losing."

"What happened was not your fault." Josie tucked a
stray curl back into her messy bun.

"If I hadn't opened my big mouth, then Evelyn
wouldn't have been provoked into sending those letters
and ole Willy Banks wouldn't have pulled his funding."

"You don't know that. Evelyn has been vocal since
Zoe's arrest."

A dull ache pulsed in the pit of Agnes's stomach. "Ian

was so upset. I need to do something to show how sorry I am."

"You're doing it again, Agnes. Ian isn't Bobby. His love isn't conditional." Josie moved out of the dining room and headed for the kitchen.

Agnes followed. "I screwed up, Josie."

"No, you didn't. Ian cares for you. This is going to blow over."

As promised, she'd told Josie the other day what was going on with Ian, but had asked her to keep it to herself. Agnes and Ian had decided to keep their focus on finishing Agape House. She had, however, enjoyed their stolen moments together.

"Okay, enough of my bellyaching. Are you sure a silent auction is the best way to do this?"

"Yes, we'll keep the auction going until eight o'clock, which will give everyone all day to bid. Once the auction ends, we'll sort through the bids and determine who won each item. We can call them tomorrow and remind them they have twenty-four hours to pay and pick up their furniture."

"Do you think we'll raise much?"

"Agnes, anything will be appreciated, so stop worrying."

"Are you positive you don't want a percentage of the profits?"

"No, Agape House needs all the funds. Besides, most of them people coming in to bid will want drinks and food anyway, so I'll do just fine."

The bell above the front door jangled against the glass. Agnes fixed a smile on her face, pushed through the kitchen door and headed to the dining room to begin her day.

Throughout the day, a steady stream of people came in

to browse and bid. More than once, people asked Agnes if she'd consider restoring some of the junk they'd thought about donating or throwing out.

She pressed her business cards into their hands and recommended they check out her website, then suggested they give her a call.

By the time eight o'clock rolled around, Agnes's feet ached and her bones felt like soggy toast. She locked the front door and turned the open sign to Closed. All she wanted now was to crawl under the covers and sleep for at least three days.

No chance of that happening.

Josie rubbed the small of her back and sighed loudly as she settled onto the couch in front of the fireplace. Kicking off her shoes, she said, "Let's finish this thing."

"You go home. I can tally the bids."

"Are you kidding? I'm excited to see how much money your pieces brought in. Who knows—maybe it will be a new fund-raising idea for other organizations."

Half an hour later, Josie punched the final number into her calculator, then grinned. "Way to go, Agnes! You scored three thousand dollars. Congratulations!"

"Are you serious?" Agnes gave her a quick hug. "Thanks, I couldn't have done it without you."

Someone tapped on the front door. Agnes looked up to find Ian peering in the window. A rush of butterflies danced in the pit of her stomach.

Avoiding Ian's eyes, she unlocked the door and let him in. "What are you doing here?"

"I tried calling, but I got your voice mail."

"My battery died. My charger is at home. I'm tired and need to finish up here, so…" She trailed off, letting him determine his next move.

"Mind if I wait and take you home? I'd like to talk."

"Fine." She turned and waved a hand toward the couch and two matching chairs set in a semicircle in front of the fireplace. "Feel free to sit. I'll be a few more minutes."

"If you two will excuse me, I'm going to finish up in the kitchen." Josie pushed off the couch, slid her feet back in her shoes and headed for the kitchen.

Instead of sitting, Ian wandered into the side dining room and ran his hand across a stenciled dresser. "What's going on in here?"

Agnes pressed a hand to her stomach. Would he think her idea was silly? Pitiful? "We had an all-day silent auction with all the proceeds benefitting Agape House."

"Why?"

She shrugged. "I felt bad about Wally Banks pulling his contributions, so I wanted to do something to help out a little."

"Red, you've done so much for Agape House already. This was totally unnecessary. Where'd this stuff come from?"

"Pieces I had sitting around in Mama's garage. I had some time on my hands the past couple of days."

He reached out and grabbed her arms. Instead of letting go, he slid his hands around her shoulders. "I can't believe you did all of this practically overnight."

She kept her hands on his forearms, still feeling a little wounded by his words the other day. "Why not? My big mouth can be used for good, too, you know."

He released her and stepped back. "I'm sorry. I was a jerk for what I said."

"Yes, you were." Why let him off the hook so easily? "You really need to loosen up, Ian."

"I can't just sit back and do nothing." He shoved his hands in the front pockets of his khaki shorts and walked to the window overlooking Main Street. A muscle jumped in the side of his jaw.

She walked behind him and placed a hand on his back. "No one's saying that, but you can't freak out every time something doesn't go according to plan. I'm going to finish up so we can get out of here and head home."

He turned and grinned. "I love the sound of that."

She gave him a playful punch in the shoulder, but didn't deny she did, too. "You know what I mean."

Less than half an hour later, Ian pulled into her driveway and shifted the engine into Park. Then he hurried around and opened her door, extending a hand to help her out. "Want to walk down to the dock?"

She stood by his SUV and rested her head on his shoulder. "I'd love to, but I'm so exhausted. Today was a long day."

"There's always tomorrow."

She loved the sound of that.

He wrapped an arm around her shoulder and ushered her to the door. She pulled his head toward her and kissed him. "Good night, Ian."

"Good night, love." Silhouetted by the moon, Ian walked back to his SUV, started it, then disappeared into the night.

The simple endearment provided a soothing balm to her wounded spirit.

Chapter Thirteen

Attending the Shelby Lake Founder's Day Celebration with Ian shouldn't have been a big deal. After all, they'd attended the parade, the carnival and fireworks together since she was twelve.

As friends, though, not a couple.

With so many people around, privacy was impossible. She appreciated Ian making an effort not to publicize their relationship. Although he did do the occasional hand graze and take advantage to whisper in her ear.

They stood in the shade of the carousel and waved at Josie and Nick sitting on one of the benches holding Noah between them while Hannah rode a purple horse with stars on its mane.

The sweet smell of cotton candy and candied apples mingled with the grease from the French fry stand, making her mouth water.

Two teen girls from her Sunday school wearing denim shorts with cowboy boots passed by and waved. They rushed in line for the Tilt-A-Whirl behind a couple of cute guys.

Agnes remembered those days.

Screams from the adventurous spirits on the roller

coaster swarmed over their heads as young children on the miniature fire trucks circled a small track.

Agnes pinched off a piece of the pink cotton candy and stuffed it in her mouth, savoring the melting sugar on her tongue. "You sure you don't want any?"

"No, thanks. That's a toothache waiting to happen."

"You're no fun. Nothing wrong with indulging in a little sugar."

"I'm all for a little sugar." He winked and gave her a slow grin that sent warmth crawling across her cheeks. "You go ahead. I'm holding out for an elephant ear."

"Those things will clog your arteries."

"Hey, you got what you wanted. Now it's my turn."

The calliope music battled with the heckles of the carnival workers trying to get someone to step up and take a chance at their game.

"Hey, man. Come and win a prize for your girl."

Ian wrapped an arm around Agnes's shoulder. "She's got the best prize of all, pal."

A sensation skittered down her spine.

The carousel stopped.

Hannah tugged on her arm. "Aggie, wanna go on the Ferris wheel with us?"

Agnes looked across the midway at the giant ride, staring down at her. Her last bite of cotton candy stuck in her throat.

Ian glanced at her, then grabbed Hannah's hand and twirled her. "What if you ride the bumper cars with me? We can team up against your dad and Red."

"Ferris wheel first, then bumper cars. Say yes. Pleeeease."

Unable to resist the endearing brown eyes pleading with her, Agnes followed the Brennans to the ride. She hated the Ferris wheel and forced herself not to dig her heels into the grass.

"You don't have to do this. We can do something else. Maybe even the fun house." Ian turned her in the direction of the weirdly shaped wacky shack.

"No, I'll go." The past couple of months had been about facing her fears, so why stop now. She could do this, especially with Ian by her side.

She tucked her hand in his arm and dragged him back in line for the Ferris wheel. Hannah found one of her friends. The two girls chattered like hyper chipmunks.

"Look—she's found a friend. Offer to take pictures of them up there or something."

Agnes shielded her eyes and tilted her head back to stare at the top of the ride. "I'll be fine as long as you're with me."

"I'm always here for you, Red. You know that."

When their turn came, they climbed three steps and sat on the open chair. The ride operator snapped the safety bar across them. The metal seats, warmed by the afternoon sunshine, heated her legs. When the seat jerked as they moved backward, Agnes gripped the safety bar.

"You okay?" Ian slung an arm over her shoulder. His fingers caressed her upper arm.

She paused a second, then leaned into his embrace, allowing his closeness to wrap her in a blanket of security. "Yeah, I'm fine."

"As long as you're not about to be sick or anything."

"Heights don't bother me. It's the confined space I have a problem with." She peered over her shoulder and waved to Hannah and her friend. "I never told you this because I was embarrassed, but in ninth grade, Gary Connolly invited me to the fair.

"I remember that. When I asked you about it, you bit my head off."

"Yeah, well, a girl doesn't like being made a fool. We got stuck at the top of the Ferris wheel when a kid got sick. Gary tried to use the situation to his advantage and about lost a hand. When the ride ended, he ditched me. Said I wasn't worth it and went off with another girl. I had to call Daddy for a ride home. I haven't been on the Ferris wheel since that awful night."

Ian shifted in his seat, causing their chair to rock. "Red, I have a confession."

"What's that?" As the ride moved them around, the breeze cooled her warm face.

"I overheard Gary bragging about what happened. I knew the jerk was lying. I confronted him and told him to keep his mouth shut. He swung at me, so I decked him."

"That was you? You never said anything."

Agnes leaned back against him and allowed the confession to sink in. Her protector. He'd never let anything happen to her. "My dragon slayer."

"He ratted me out to my dad." Ian shook his head and chuckled. "Dad commended me for defending your honor but made it clear we don't solve our problems with our fists."

"Oh, Ian. I don't know what to say." Her vision blurred as she glanced down at her hands in her lap, but she blinked back wetness, thankful for her sunglasses.

He shrugged. "You don't have to say anything. It was so long ago."

"True. When my marriage fell apart, Bobby said I wasn't worth it either. And, well, when you hear something more than once, you tend to believe it...." Her voice trailed off with the wind.

"Agnes, don't let him get inside your head. You are so worth it. You're amazing."

"I'm not amazing, Ian. I'm just a thro—"

He pressed his finger to her lips and lowered his voice. "Don't say it. You're not a throwaway."

She wrapped her fingers around his and squeezed gently. "Everyone should have someone like you in their lives. I'm glad you're in mine."

"I meant what I said about measuring every man by Bobby's yardstick. I promise no one will hurt you like that again."

"Mama always said, 'A *promise* is a big word. It either makes something or breaks everything.'"

"I mean every word."

"That's what makes you special—you don't go back on your word. My next husband will know the true meaning of promise because the poor sap'll be stuck with me for the rest of his life."

"Your next husband, huh? I'd be more than willing to take on that role."

The seat jerked as the Ferris wheel came to a stop. Agnes's stomach tumbled. From the ride or Ian's admission? His words sent a spark to her heart. But life as Ian's wife still felt so out of reach.

"When you realize what a great person you are, I'll be waiting to say, 'I told you so.'"

The sky exploded with spheres of red, blue and silver. As the final fireworks crackled and drifted down, their group stood and shook out blankets.

Nick hoisted sleeping Noah on his shoulder—how the kid slept through the fireworks amazed Ian—while Josie gathered their things and folded their blanket. Lindsey cradled Thomas while Stephen lifted Gracie Ann.

Seeing them gather their families created an ache in Ian's chest. Especially after his conversation with Red on the Ferris wheel.

He wanted to be more than her best friend. He wanted to be the protector of her heart. He wanted to be the love of her life.

They all bid goodbyes. Red and Ian watched them walk to their cars. She had invited everyone back to her mom's place for a late evening wiener roast and perfect view of fireworks over the lake.

The burning embers of the fire snapped and crackled as a burned log shifted, sending a shower of sparks skyward.

Lightning bugs drifted past them. He reached out and cupped one in his hands. He held it out to Red, who took it. "Remember when we used to catch these in your mom's Mason jars."

"Remember when Zoe let yours loose in your bedroom." She opened her hands and released the firefly.

"Yeah, Mom wasn't too thrilled with that. Good times. I miss them." He stuffed his hands in his front pockets and stared at the moon dripping across the sooty lake.

The night peepers serenaded them from the bank.

"Next year."

"You seem hopeful."

"Of course. What's the point of having a dream if you don't believe in it?" Red shook out the blanket they had shared. Instead of folding it, she wrapped it around her and clutched it under her chin.

"Cold?" He turned and smoothed the folds around her neck.

"A little. I should probably head inside." Yet she made no effort to move.

"Before you go…I, uh, wondered if I could ask you something?"

"Of course. You can ask me anything. You know that."

Ian shoved his left hand in his front pocket and scratched the back of his head with the other. He kicked at the grass with the toe of his beat-up deck shoe.

Agnes looked at him. "You okay? You've been quiet since we left the carnival."

He gave her a wry smile. "I'm surprised you noticed with the horde of people here."

Red let go of the blanket to fix her ponytail. As she gathered her hair and secured it, he reached forward and gently pulled her hand away. Her hair tumbled past her shoulders.

He wound a curl around his index finger. "Your hair's getting long."

"Almost long enough to cut and donate to Locks of Love. After Josie cut her hair for Hannah's wig when she battled leukemia, I decided I could grow out my hair and do the same for another little girl."

"You are incredible, you know that?"

She shook her head.

She wasn't fishing for compliments. Of course, she didn't believe in herself the way he believed in her. Thanks to that idiot she had married.

He released her hair and caressed her cheek with his thumb. "You have the softest skin."

Before she had time to react, he dipped his head and lowered his lips to hers. Her hands gripped the open collar of his button-down shirt. He deepened the kiss and wrapped his arms around her waist, drawing her close. She stood on tiptoes and slid her hands over his shoulders.

Slowly she pulled away and rested her forehead against his shirt.

He curled her into his chest and pressed his cheek to the top of her head. "I've wanted to do that all day."

Red breathed deeply, then stepped out of his embrace. "Ian, what's going on?"

"What do you mean?"

She picked up the blanket again, but instead of wrapping it around herself, she twisted it around her hands. "I don't know. I can't really explain it. You just seem... different since this afternoon. Almost like you're deep in thought about something."

He crossed his arms to keep from reaching for her again. "You remember what you said on the Ferris wheel that everyone should have someone like me in their lives?"

"Of course. And I meant it. You're the best friend I've ever had."

"I know you did. And I appreciate it, Red. I do." He exhaled and scrubbed a hand over the back of his head. "It's just...well, what if that's not good enough for me anymore?"

"Wh-what do you mean? You don't want to be with me now?" Through the trees, the moonlight highlighted the sudden glisten in her eyes.

He wasn't explaining himself very well. "No, no, Red. Relax. It's nothing like that."

"Then what?"

He was acting like a fourteen-year-old.

Just spit it out, man.

He stepped forward and cradled her face. His voice dropped to a whisper. "I meant it a couple of weeks ago when I said I love you. I do. I love being your best friend, but I want more. I want to marry you, to have a future with you...a family. When I wake up, I look forward to seeing you. When I go to bed, I drift off to sleep with you in my thoughts."

She tightened the blanket around her and took another step back, her face crumbling. "Oh, Ian…"

That was not what he wanted to hear.

He bit back a growl and fought the urge not to bang his head against the nearest tree trunk. He rubbed his eyes with his thumb and forefinger, then held up a hand. "Listen, forget it. Forget I said anything. It was stupid."

She moved toward him and placed a hand on his arm. "No, Ian—"

"Go home, Red. Thanks for today. I had a great time."

He turned and started to walk away. Heat scalded his neck and ears. At least he had the common sense to kiss her in the moonlight so he wouldn't have to see the pity in her eyes in the daylight.

"Now, you wait a doggone minute. You had your say. Now it's my turn."

He stopped, but didn't turn around. Hadn't he humiliated himself enough?

She jerked on his shoulder, forcing him to turn and face her. Even bathed in moonlight, fire blazed in her eyes. Her chest shuddered. "You don't get to lay all of that at my feet and walk way. I get to have a say, too. You promised not to rush me. You agreed to wait until we finished with Agape House. I'm still trying to get used to us, and you're talking marriage. Let a girl catch her breath."

His heart cracked a little. He brushed the backs of his fingers over her cheek, unable to keep from reaching out to her. "What makes you think it wouldn't work?"

"There are things I haven't told you. Things that could…change how you feel. I'm afraid…I don't know." She reached up and pulled his hand away from her face.

"If I lost you, I wouldn't have anything left. Can't you understand that?"

"Yes, Red, I can." A growl snarled low in his throat. He rubbed his eyes, horrified to find his fingers damp. His voice choked as he dragged her to his chest. "The day you walked down the aisle to become Mrs. Bobby Levine about ripped my guts out. For the first and only time in my life, I wanted to drink myself stupid to numb the pain. So I do have an idea what it's like to lose you.

She braced her hands against him. "You never lost me."

"I'm tired of wishing. Didn't you just tell me what's the point of having a dream if you didn't believe in it? I believe in us. And it's time I acted on that dream. I want a relationship with you. I want to marry you, Agnes. Raise a family with you."

She bit her lip and turned away. Her voice dropped to a whisper. "But what if I can't give you what you want? What if you leave and decide I'm not worth it? This scares me, Ian."

"Life is scary, but we can't run from it for fear of having our hearts broken."

"It's so much more than that."

"Then tell me…help me to understand what's holding you back. If you don't believe in us, then yeah, you could lose me. I'm not going to wait another twenty years for you to make up your mind."

She stared at him with almost violet eyes. A tear slid down the side of her face. Without a word, she turned and hurried toward her house, stumbling on the blanket tripping around her bare feet.

He'd been so sure she was ready to move forward with their relationship. Otherwise he wouldn't have flayed his chest open and exposed his heart. Now it felt as if it had been ripped out and dragged across the yard behind her.

He didn't know where to go from here. He truly didn't.

Chapter Fourteen

Agnes just wanted to get through her shift.

She had very few days where she didn't want to go to work, but today was one of those stay-in-bed-with-covers-over-her-head kind of mornings. Especially with the drizzle that ran off the Cuppa Josie's blue and brown-striped canopy over the entrance.

Mondays were her usual days off, but when Josie called and asked her to cover so she could go for a doctor's appointment, Agnes couldn't say no.

Besides, she wasn't one to tuck tail and run. But after Saturday night and replaying Ian walking away over and over in her head, she just wanted to curl up in pajama pants and watch movies all day.

If only life could be like a two-hour romantic comedy with each plot twist tied up by the time the credits rolled.

She'd even skipped church yesterday. Any other time she hadn't gone, Ian was at her door making sure she was okay. No one knocked on her door. Her phone remained silent except for a call from Mama saying she'd be home sooner than expected…something else Agnes wasn't ready for.

So maybe she was a coward yesterday to avoid Ian, but today she was spitting mad.

Two days ago, he had professed his love a second time and talked marriage, yet today he flaunted another woman right under her very nose. Drinking coffee as if he wasn't the least bit as miserable as she was.

Jerk.

Before things had gotten serious between them, she'd suggested he ask out Breena Nelson, the cute little twentysomething owner of a clothing store a block down from Cuppa Josie's, but he'd insisted he wasn't interested.

Boy, he looked pretty interested right now.

Maybe Ian was like other guys after all. Didn't get what he wanted, so he moved on.

And she was the fool to believe his sweet words.

She sprayed glass cleaner on the smoke-colored glass front door and tried to ignore Breena's annoying laugh that rivaled a hyena's. If she wiped any harder, she'd put a hole through the glass.

Ian must be oh-so funny today. Absolutely hysterical.

Agnes's shoulders hunched around her ears as Breena's high-pitched cackle bounced off the walls. She gave the window one last swipe, then stomped back to the kitchen.

Josie had returned from her appointment and stood at the stove scooping cookie dough onto a baking sheet. "What's wrong?"

"Nothing." Agnes dropped the window cleaner and paper towels on the counter, then washed her hands, keeping her back to Josie.

"What's going with you and Ian?"

"Nothing."

Oh, boy. Did that ring true or what?

"On Saturday, the guy couldn't keep his eyes off you, but now he's drinking coffee with Breena."

Agnes whirled around, facing Josie, and fought back the tears scalding her eyes. "Sugar Pie, that boy doesn't have a lick of sense when it comes to women."

Josie scooped some cookie dough into a small dish and handed it to Agnes. "That *man* definitely knows what he wants, and it's about time he went after it."

"Apparently what he thought he wanted wasn't what he really wanted after all." Agnes scooped out cookie dough with her finger and put it in her mouth.

"When Nick returned to town a couple of years ago and tried to get back together, you reminded me he had been showing his love by what he did for me and I wasn't listening with my heart." Josie leaned against the counter and pointed at Agnes with her cookie scoop. "I'm throwing your words back at you. I know you're scared. I get that. I was, too. Even though he drives me nuts at times, I can't imagine my life without him. You have to decide if you're willing to take that same risk with Ian."

Chewing on Josie's words, Agnes returned to the dining room. Then wished she had stayed in the kitchen.

Breena had her hand on Ian's arm, and the fool didn't bother moving it. The way she smiled at him…and that pink sleeveless dress with the white heels…positively indecent.

Actually she looked rather cute. In fact, Agnes hated to admit just how well Ian and Breena looked together.

Her heart sagged with the weight of a thundercloud.

Rising from his chair, Ian laughed at something she said and carried their cups to the coffee bar to refill them.

He pressed the air pot labeled Pecan Pie Cream, but it dribbled into the cup. "Red, coffee's out."

"I can see that with my own eyes, Ian James."

He raised an eyebrow at her sharp tone. She snagged the air pot off the counter and carried it into the kitchen to swap it out for a fresh one.

She stomped back to the dining room and slammed the air pot on the counter. "Now you have a fresh pot."

She started to walk away, then stormed back to him, poking him in the chest. "You know, I wanted you to try this blend for weeks, but you kept saying it wasn't for you. Now that you've tried it, you're coming back for more. Makes me wonder if you're even going to want your regular coffee anymore."

Ian set the cup on the counter and reached for her hand, pulling it away from his chest. A muscle jumped in the side of his jaw. "I don't know. Maybe I'm looking for something more. Maybe a little spice to kick my regular coffee up a notch."

She glanced at Breena, who had her back to them, texting. "Well, enjoy the special. I hope it's worth it."

He dragged a hand over his face. "One special, Red. This one's a little too sweet for my taste, but I tried it."

Agnes moved behind the register and wet a clean dishcloth in the small sink. She returned to the coffee counter to wipe up spilled sugar. She had to do something, anything to put a little distance between them. "What if you stay with your usual and decide down the road that it's stale and boring, and you want something new?"

Ian pressed his hands on her shoulders and turned her gently until she was pinned between him and the counter. "You know why I order the same coffee morning after morning?"

She shook her head, trying not to melt into his touch. Why did he have to smell like fresh air after a spring rain? Why did his broad shoulders have to lure her into a sense of security? Why did he have to ruin everything by falling in love?

He lowered his voice and caressed her cheek. "It's bold, exciting. That first beautiful sip helps me get through the rest of the day. After all these years if you think I'm going to order something new, then you don't know me very well."

"You're bound to change your mind. Then Josie's going to be stuck with old, stale coffee with no purpose."

He took a step back and shoved his hands in his pockets. The light in his eyes dimmed. "I love my old, boring coffee very much. I wanted to spend the rest of my life drinking the same rich, delicious blend, but now I'm wondering if it's even available anymore."

What could she say to that?

"Are you going to start seeing Breena?"

Ian rubbed a hand across his jaw. "No, Red. Breena called my office and asked if we could meet here about an insurance issue. It's all business."

"Ian—"

The front door opened, the bells at the top of the door clanging against the glass.

Agnes swallowed her words and scooted behind the counter. What she had to say needed to wait. She had a customer to wait on.

A man with short dark hair and a trimmed beard entered. Something about his size and stance reminded her of someone, but his baseball cap shaded the upper portion of his face.

He wore clean jeans, tan work boots and a yellow T-shirt with a logo on the left breast pocket. He strode to the counter.

Her breath caught in her throat, threatening to squeeze

her windpipe. She gripped the edge of the counter. A tremble started at her toes and spread through her body.

Oh, dear God, no...

A wide smile creased the man's tanned face. "Agnes Levine, you look even prettier than the day I married you."

Just when she thought the pieces of her heart had been cemented back into place, her past returned and shattered it with the force of a wrecking ball.

"B-bobby. What are you doing here?" Her eyes darted over his shoulder. Ian watched them with narrowed eyes.

Bobby followed her gaze and nodded to Ian, who didn't reciprocate. He directed his gaze at her, smiling wide. "Why, sweetheart, I've come to win you back."

Outside, thunderclouds rolled and echoed through the valley as lightning electrified the air. But that was nothing compared to the storm surge inside the building.

The absurdity of his comment made her shake her head.

She hadn't seen Bobby in almost six years. And all that time she'd rehearsed what she'd say if she saw him again. Words hovered on her tongue, but the courage to speak disappeared.

Her eyes darted around the room, looking for a quick escape. No, she wouldn't run. Those days were over. For weeks, she'd been confronting the past. She wasn't about to lose it in front of him now.

She pulled in a lungful of air, then exhaled quietly. Maybe ignoring his comment would be best.

Pasting her customer smile in place, she looked at him again.

"What can I get for you?"

He glanced at the chalkboard advertising the specials. "Just coffee to go."

Agnes handed him a foam to-go cup and lid hoping he couldn't see her trembling fingers. "Coffee's on the counter. Help yourself."

"Do you have a minute to talk?"

"I'm working, Bobby." Over his shoulder, she saw Ian and Breena laughed about something, then Breena gathered her purse and umbrella before heading for the door. Ian returned to his chair and sipped his coffee, his eyes not leaving Bobby.

"What about later? After your shift ends? I'm in town overnight and would like to see you before I head back home."

She swallowed and willed her body to stop shaking. "I'm not so sure that would be a good idea."

He pulled out a business card, scribbled a number on the back and slid it across the counter to her. "Here's my cell. Give me a call if you change your mind."

Once he moved to the coffee counter with his cup, Ian strode to the register. "What's he doing here?"

"He wants to talk to me after work." Her voice sounded vacant as she watched the man who had inflicted so much damage on her heart and soul.

"Are you going to?"

"I don't know. I'm kind of curious as to what he has to say."

"I don't like it, Red. Not one bit." His lips thinned as lines pinched his mouth. "You're not to see him alone. Got it?"

"First of all, Ian, you're not my boss. Second, I'm not so crazy about it myself, but I'm tired of being afraid of my past."

"If he hurts you—"

"He won't." She didn't know why, but something seemed different about Bobby. She couldn't figure it out.

Ian glared at Bobby's back as he gripped the counter. Agnes's hand shot out and grabbed his arm. "Relax, Ian."

Bobby snapped the lid on his steaming cup and winked at Agnes. "Catch you later, Agnes." He headed for the door.

"No, Red. That guy hurt you. I'm going to make sure he doesn't do it again." Ian shook off Agnes's hand and strode after Bobby.

Oh, boy.

Agnes rounded the side of the counter and rushed across the room, her heart thumping against her ribs.

"You touch her again, and you'll answer to me."

Bobby drew himself to his full height, but Ian still towered over him by several inches. He scoffed. "No reason to worry, Ian. I'll be out of here before you know it."

"Good riddance, Levine. Don't let me stop you." Ian fisted his hands.

"Don't worry, James, I never let you stop me from doing anything."

Agnes jumped between the two of them and pushed Ian back. She glared at Bobby. "Knock it off. Both of you. This competition to see who's the better man ends now."

Ian snaked an arm around her waist and pulled her close, banging her hip against his thigh. "No competition, Red. We know who the winner is."

She loved being close to Ian, but not like this. She pushed Ian's arm off her and whirled around, poking a finger in his chest. "Back off. I didn't ask you to come over to him."

Crimson flared up his neck to his hairline. His jaw clenched as his eyes turned to steel. He released her and stepped back, nodding to her and Bobby. "You're right. The mighty Agnes Kingsley doesn't need anyone fighting her battles for her. Heaven forbid if someone got close enough to actually penetrate that wall you've built."

"Ian, don't be ridiculous." She reached for his arm. "That's not what I meant and you know it."

He jerked back as if he had been stung by her touch. Backing up, he put his hands up. "Forget it, Red. I'm done. This…" He circled the area between the three of them. "It's not worth it." Then he turned and pushed through the front door so hard it smacked against the outer brick wall.

The glass door remained unharmed, but her heart? It shattered into a million little shards.

Ian scrubbed a hand over his face where the pulses of humiliation dug deep into his skin. He was tired. So tired of fighting. So tired of not measuring up against Bobby Levine.

He gripped the steering wheel so tightly his knuckles whitened and his joints protested. He'd love nothing more than to rearrange the jerk's face. He couldn't leave town fast enough. Then Ian wouldn't have to worry about him messing with Red.

She'd humiliated him in front of Bobby.

Just once Ian wanted to walk away the victor.

But today, he'd just walked away.

An ache pounded behind his eyes. Trying to navigate in the driving rain didn't help either.

His cell phone chirped from the cup holder in the console. Ian pulled into a parking space and saw Dad's number on the screen. He answered. "Dad. What's up?"

"Ian. Need you to get over to Agape House. Pronto." Dad's voice sounded hollow, and with the wind whistling, his words were tough to make out.

Ian snapped off the radio and plugged his other ear to try and hear better. "What's wrong?"

"There's been some storm damage."

His blood turned to ice, chilling his veins. "How bad?"

"I think you need to see for yourself."

Ian didn't like the sound of that. He shifted into gear and headed for Agape House.

He pulled into the driveway behind his parents' sedan. Mom wore a rain slicker and huddled under an umbrella. No sign of Dad or Griffin. Both had been asleep when he left this morning.

He circled to the back of his SUV, opened the lift-gate and jammed his feet into heavy socks and work boots he had tossed in this morning for working at Agape House once the rain let up. He thrust his arms through a red James & Son Windbreaker, closed up the SUV and jogged across the wet grass to Mom.

Rain pelted his face. He ducked under Mom's umbrella and took it from her, shielding both of them. "What's going on?"

Seeing him, she turned and buried her face in his chest but jerked a thumb over her shoulder.

Then he saw it.

Handing back the umbrella, he strode to the side of the house, his boots crunching on broken branches. As he looked up, air escaped through his lungs, leaving him feeling boneless and hopeless.

The very tree he planned to cut the other day cleaved the peak over the attached garage. The front punched-out window frame lay in a shower of broken glass on the driveway.

Bile slicked the back of his throat. This couldn't be happening.

Ian stared, then squeezed his eyes shut. Maybe, just

maybe, his eyes had played tricks on him. Maybe what he saw was a figment of his imagination.

Drawing in a deep breath, he opened his eyes.

No optic tricks. No figments of his imagination.

The tree still split the center of the roof.

He had enough experience as a claims adjuster to know the damage wouldn't be cheap to repair. And there was no way it could be fixed in time for next week's open house.

They had been so close.

Without Agape House, would the parole board agree to releasing Zoe?

Thunder rattled through the trees like giant marbles across a wooden floor.

Clenching his fists, he wanted to pound something, anything to detract from the pain in his chest.

Tears burned his eyes.

All he wanted was his family back together.

Was that too much to ask, God? Huh, was it?

They'd hit so many roadblocks that maybe this was God's final way of saying to forget it and walk away. Was he so consumed by his own desires that he tuned out God's?

Dad stomped through the yard over to Ian. Rain dripped from the brim of his ball cap. "Grab your camera and get pictures taken. I'm going to send your mother to Ernie's hardware store to get tarps and plastic. We need to batten down that roof to avoid more damage."

"Where's Griffin?"

"He's at Jimmy's."

Ian retrieved his Canon from the SUV and started snapping photos for the insurance claim.

Mom must've have called in the troops or something, because cars and trucks arrived. Doors slammed as people poured across the yard carrying ladders. Within seconds, chain saws whined through the tree as the winds howled at the injustice of the damage.

For the next hour, they cut the fallen tree in chunks and removed it from the roof.

Ladders picketed the side and front of the house as a group of guys hauled large tarps to the roof and secured them over the peak to minimalize water damage.

Ian dragged his hands through his soaked hair and smashed a ball cap backward on his head to keep his hair out of his eyes. He kicked broken glass away with the side of his boot and leaned the ladder against the front of the house, then climbed to staple plastic where the window had been.

An eerie light sliced through the room above the garage, casting shadows on the floor. Even with the wind and rain, the scent of paint and promise lingered. But now, the tree split their hopes, their dreams, claiming victory.

Swallowing the defeat climbing up his throat, he focused on preventing more water from blowing into the room. As he stretched out his arm to hold the end of the plastic with one hand so he could staple it with the other, the ladder shifted and skidded on the wet cement.

He reached for the window frame, but the wooden structure slipped from his wet grasp. His hands clawed the air as the trees and sky jerked out of reach.

He landed in the grass with a dull thud. Air whooshed from his lungs like compressed bellows.

The blurry images of the trees, the sky, the ladder faded as darkness chased away the blinding light.

Chapter Fifteen

Not worth it.

No matter how busy she stayed, those three words played on a continuous loop inside Agnes's head.

Ian broke the promise he made that afternoon on the Ferris wheel.

He said he'd never hurt her, but he did. And their relationship wouldn't be the same again.

How was she going to recover from that?

With arms folded over her chest, Agnes stared out the picture window at Cuppa Josie's as the wind swept the rain across the pavement. Limbs and leaves stumbled along the sidewalk. Cars crawled down the streets.

Behind her, the dining room remained empty. The ticking clock above the fireplace echoed off the ice-blue walls.

People had taken shelter against the storm. Josie called from the doctor's office, urging her to lock up and leave.

Only problem was, she didn't have a ride with her car still at Buck's Garage. So she was stuck here until the storm died down enough for her to walk home.

She wasn't calling Ian. Not when he'd made it clear they were done.

Not worth it.

Losing her best friend scraped her heart raw, exposing every wound and leaving her in misery.

Even though he'd been gone only a couple of hours, she missed him.

She missed feeling her phone vibrate in her pocket as he sent her a random text. She missed knowing he was only around the corner...well, maybe he was holed up in his office, waiting out the storm, but she didn't know that because she hadn't heard from him since he slammed the door, dragging her heart behind him.

A tear trickled down her cheek.

If only she could have a do-over, take back her words and handle that whole situation differently.

Then she wouldn't be feeling like one of those leaves being tossed by the storm.

Too bad life didn't come with do-overs.

A noise from the kitchen pulled her attention away from the front window. As she walked through the dining room to investigate, Josie and Nick burst through the door, laughing and snapping each other playfully with towels.

"Hey, what are you two doing out in this weather?"

Josie snatched Nick's towel from him and dropped it on the counter next to the register. "We were on our way home from the doctor's and saw the lights. We wanted to make sure everything was okay. I needed to talk to you anyway, so now we can chat face-to-face."

"About what?"

Their exchanged glances did little to ease the tension in Agnes's spine. Then Josie smiled and headed behind the counter. "First I need some tea."

"Sit, sweetheart. I'll get it." Nick dropped a kiss on

Josie's head and brushed a hand over her damp hair. "Want anything, Agnes?"

She shook her head. "I'm good, but thanks."

Josie pulled Agnes over to the couch, plopped on a couch, then patted the one beside her. "Have a seat, Agnes."

"What's going on?"

Josie folded her hands over her growing belly and rested her feet on the coffee table in front of her. "I'm… well, we're having twins." The smile on her face spread faster than melted chocolate.

Agnes leaned over and hugged her friend. "That's great! Congratulations. Nick may be getting that football team after all."

Josie blinked back tears and threaded her fingers together. "But there's something else."

Thunder rolled and echoed through the valley, shaking the building. A flash of lightning caused the lights to flicker.

"There are some slight complications. The doctor has ordered me to take it easy." She glanced at Agnes through her fringed lashes.

Agnes put a hand on her arm. "Are you okay?"

"Yes, as long as I slow down."

"Does your doctor realize who he has for a patient?"

Josie nodded toward the counter. "Yeah, well, Watchdog Nick promised to look after me."

Nick returned at that moment, carrying two mugs. He set one in front of his wife; then he settled on one of the side chairs. The scent of vanilla drifted over them. "Your health and our unborn babies are my priorities."

Josie took a sip of tea, then set it on the coffee table. She glanced at Nick. "Nick and I talked. Then on the way home, I called Dad and Grace. Now that they're both retired, they're willing to take over Cuppa Josie's for an undetermined amount of time."

Agnes regretted turning down the offer of tea. She needed something to do with her hands. She picked up one of the throw pillows and hugged it to her chest. "What do you mean by taking over?"

Josie shifted so she faced her friend. "I mean they will be running the business instead of me. Grace will do the baking, and Dad's going to take over the business end of things."

"So you won't be here at all?"

"No."

The single word felt like a punch in the stomach.

Josie pressed a hand on Agnes's knee. "But don't worry, Agnes—your job is totally safe."

That was the last thing she was worried about at the moment. "Thanks for that, but it won't be quite the same without you."

"I'm sorry." Josie reached for her tea again, but not before Agnes caught a flicker of sadness.

"No, don't apologize. I didn't mean to heap a big ole scoop of guilt on your head. Just making a comment. So, when will they take over?" Agnes rushed to put her friend at ease, feeling awful for her selfish thinking. Of course Josie needed to take care of herself.

"You like Dad and Grace, right?" The look in Josie's eyes pleaded for her to understand and accept the new changes.

Agnes forced a smile on her face and laughed. "Oh, absolutely, Sugar Pie."

Josie released a sigh and rested her head against the back of the couch. "Good, because they adore you. My dad thinks you're feisty. They will be here on Monday. I'm going to spend a couple of hours with them each day to help them get a feel for everything, but then Nick is insisting I go home and limit my activities."

Agnes stared out the window at the rain pelting the flowers ringing the ornamental trees planted near the curb. Even though rain coursed down the petals, the stems kept them strong…kept them from lying in the muddy mulch…exhausted from defeat.

Josie and Nick needed her. They counted on her. And she needed to buck up and be the friend they deserved.

"Now, don't you worry another minute. Between your daddy and Grace, we'll keep this place going with no problem."

Tears filled Josie's eyes. "You are the most amazing friend. You know that?"

"You stop that crying, or ole Nick'll have two blubbering females on his hands. And what guy wants that?" Agnes succeeded in making Josie laugh and drying her eyes.

Agnes gathered Josie's and Nick's empty mugs and carried them to the kitchen sink, needing a few minutes to process without an audience. As she wet a sponge and added a drop of dish soap, she let the tears flow down her face.

So many changes in everyone else's lives, but hers felt empty. Did God decide after thirty-six years of trying, she simply wasn't worth the effort anymore?

She wanted to call Ian and share this new information about Josie and Nick, but he wouldn't want to be bothered. She could call Mama, but after talking to her the other day, she knew Mama was busy moving Memaw into her new apartment.

She'd power through this by herself. After all, relying on others created unnecessary heartache. And she couldn't handle one more thing today.

The kitchen door opened. "You about ready, Agnes?"

Agnes nodded and tried to keep her voice light. "Yes, give me another minute."

"You okay? Your voice sounds funny."

Agnes didn't even bother to cover her face. She gripped the edge of the sink and dropped her head as sobs shook her shoulders. "He doesn't want me, Josie. Said I wasn't worth it."

"Oh, Agnes. I'm so sorry." Josie wrapped an arm around her shoulder. "What happened?"

Agnes dried her eyes with the back of her hand and reached for a paper towel. She relayed the events of the past few weeks, ending with Ian walking out. "If there's damage to the door, I'll pay for it."

"Seriously, Agnes? I don't care about that. I care about you. Ian loves you. He's mad. Let him blow off steam, and he'll come around. Remember what I went through with Nick? Why don't you come home with us for the afternoon? You can hear about Hannah's latest friend drama and snuggle up with Noah. We can find a chick flick and make homemade pizza."

"Thanks, Sugar Pie. I think I'll take you up on that."

"Great, I'll have Nick turn out the lights in the dining room while you grab your stuff."

The coffee shop phone rang, but Josie must have grabbed it in the dining room since the ringing stopped before Agnes could reach it.

Josie pushed through the kitchen door, her face drained of color.

"What's wrong?"

She held out the phone. "Pete's on the line for you."

Agnes took the phone. "Hello?"

"Agnes Joy, it's Pete."

"What's up?"

"We're at the emergency room. Ian fell off a ladder. He's unconscious, but no broken bones." Pete's voice choked.

To hear Pete lose it sent a tremor through her body. Her heart tumbled down her chest, knocking off each rib before smashing at her feet. She shot a glance at Josie.

Josie reached for her hands. "We will take you to the hospital."

"I'm on my way, Pete."

Ian had to be okay. He had to. She couldn't imagine life without him.

Chapter Sixteen

Josie was right—she needed to decide if she was willing to risk her heart with Ian.

Seeing him in that exam room, his skin as pasty as the sheets, nearly did her in.

Thankfully he'd suffered only a concussion. Once she knew he was out of danger, she slipped away.

Time to put the past where it belonged so she could focus on her future. Even if it didn't include Ian.

And that's the only reason she agreed to talk to Bobby.

She was tired of fighting it. Tired of lying to herself. When she called, she asked if he could extend his stay until that evening. Apparently what he wanted to say was important enough for him to agree to do it.

Now Agnes stood on Mama's deck and tried to avoid looking in the direction of the James property line.

When Agnes told Nick and Josie about Bobby wanting to talk, they insisted on being close by, so they hung out in Mama's living room while she headed for the backyard.

She breathed a prayer of protection, although she wasn't quite sure who needed it most—she or Bobby.

Bobby wouldn't hurt her.

Not here. Not now.

She didn't have proof to back up her instincts, but something about him seemed different...calmer...more mature.

Might as well get this over with.

Carrying two glasses of sweet tea, Agnes crossed the yard to the koi pond where Bobby sat in one of the white Adirondack chairs. The last thing she wanted was to be hospitable, but Mama's voice inside her head reminded her of those Southern-bred manners.

The wet grass from yesterday's downpour coated her bare feet. Sunlight elbowed its way through the storm clouds to cast a glow across the yard.

Her heart quaked with each step.

She handed Bobby a cold glass, then sat opposite him, keeping her eyes fixed on the fat fish in the pond.

Resting her elbows on the chair arms, she held the glass with two hands. "So, what did you want to talk about, Bobby?"

He downed half his glass, then set it on the grass next to his chair. He cleared his throat. "First off, I have a confession—I didn't return to Shelby Lake to win you back."

Of course not. He didn't want her the first time around, so why would he bother again? Not that she wanted him back, but his blatant rejection still stung a little.

"Then why did you say it?" She didn't mean to snap, but his presence had her on edge.

"I couldn't miss a chance to ruffle Ian's feathers."

She wanted to smack that grin off his face. "Grow up, Bobby. That stupid rivalry is in the past."

Maybe this was a mistake.

He cleared the smile from his face and schooled his

expression into a more serious one. "I have grown up, Agnes. A lot in the past five years."

"Too bad you couldn't have done it while we were still married."

"I know. And I'm sorry." He leaned forward, resting his elbows on his knees and rubbed his palms together. "For everything. You put your heart into our marriage. I didn't even meet you halfway. I can't take back what happened."

As she sat across from him, digesting his words, appreciating the truth he seemed to realize too late.

She took in his buzzed hair and trimmed beard. Apparently he took greater pride in his appearance now than when they were married. Then she caught a glint on his left hand. Something she didn't notice before.

"You're married."

Bobby glanced at the plain gold band on his left hand as a slow smile stretched across his face—one of those kinds of smiles that simply couldn't be constrained.

Agnes lowered her glass to the ground for fear of dropping it and spilling tea all over her lap. "You're in love with her."

"Of course I am. Her name's Wendy. We met about three and a half years ago."

"Where?"

"Would you believe her dad's church? We were in a singles Bible study together. One night I asked her out for coffee. Things progressed from there. We've been married for two years."

"You went to church?"

"Go figure, huh? After what happened…with you, I guess you could say I hit bottom. I went on a three-day bender, passed out in a park and ended up in the hospital with alcohol poisoning. Once I was released, I checked into rehab to dry out. Longest thirty days of my life." He reached into his front pocket and flipped a coin to her.

She caught it and recognized it as a sobriety chip. Daddy used to carry one in his pocket, too. "How long have you been sober?"

"Four years."

"Congratulations."

"Thanks. Wendy's dad, Tim, is a pastor, who visited me in rehab and led me to the Lord. Can you believe it?" Tears glossed his green eyes. He sniffed and ran a hand under his nose. "A drunk like me who used to hurt the one woman he promised to cherish? What could God want with me? I fought it for a while, but Tim's words soaked in."

Tears welled in her eyes...she couldn't help it. His vulnerability nicked at the wall she'd built to protect herself from being hurt again. The man who sat beside her might have resembled the same one whose angry shouts bounced off the walls and struck out at her, whittling away at her self-esteem. But he wasn't the same person she married.

No, with his clear eyes and clean-cut appearance, he wore redemption with grateful ease.

She pulled her knees to her chest and buried her face, allowing the resentment gurgling deep inside to well up and overflow. She wanted to lash out at him. Ask what was so wrong with her that he couldn't change while being married to her.

Her heart hung like a rusty gate.

How many times had she asked him to come to worship with her? How many times had she sat in that pew alone and tried not to envy the many couples that populated the congregation? How many times had she prayed to God to change his heart?

Why hadn't God listened?

But it seems He had. Just not in time to save her marriage.

Apparently she wasn't worth either of their efforts.

"It wasn't you."

She popped her head up to find him kneeling in front of her chair. He reached for her hand, and she tensed.

He must've felt her anxiety because he released her hand but stayed in front of her. "Agnes, you are an amazing woman. I was the screwup in our marriage."

Her chest shuddered. She stared over his head at the slice of water against the horizon, trying to keep her eyes from filling.

She had wasted emotional energy on him for years. Ian was right—he wasn't worth a minute more. But try as she might, she couldn't harness the pain that threaded her words. "Why couldn't you change for me? Why couldn't you love me?"

Bobby dragged his hands through his hair. "I don't know. I spent so much time trying to figure it out. When I think of the way I treated you, it makes me sick. I don't deserve it, but I hope you can forgive me someday."

Forgive?

Him?

The few bruises he had caused had faded years ago, but what about the ones deeply imprinted on her soul? The ones that reminded her she was nothing more than a throwaway?

The hollow spot in her womb was a constant reminder of his destruction of their marriage. And he wanted her to forgive him? For depriving her of a future? How could she do that?

"Is that why you're here? To get my forgiveness so

you can go on your merry way and have a happy life?" Bitterness tainted her words.

He stared at her a moment, then shook his head. "No. I'm ashamed to say, but it's taken me this long to find the courage to face you. Making amends is part of the recovery process, but I kept putting it off. Like I said, my past actions make me sick. I wasn't the kind of husband you deserved."

"What does your wife say about all of this?"

"She knows every sordid detail. I don't keep secrets from her. She encouraged me to come and see you. We needed to close this door, so she and I can raise our family with no regret."

"Family? You have children?" Her voice caught.

"Not quite. Wendy is four months pregnant. She's due before Christmas."

The irony slashed her core.

The cracks and crevices that had been patched around her heart split open. An ache carved out a crater in her chest so quickly she gasped for breath.

A sob clogged her throat, but she kept swallowing until she could speak without losing her composure.

With stiffened limbs, she forced herself to her feet. "Thank you for coming, Bobby. I appreciate the apology. I wish you well with your new life."

Bobby pulled out his wallet, removing a folded piece of paper. He held it out to her. "This is to repay you for the gambling debts and credit cards I racked up and left you with."

Agnes took it, unfolded the check and read the amount. The paper nearly fluttered through her fingers as she sucked in a breath. With wide eyes, she looked at him. "Where did you get this money?"

"I worked for it. Construction work pays well, especially when you're working sixty to eighty hours a week."

After Bobby left, she had worked with a debt consolidation program to pay off his online gambling debts and credit cards. She'd lived on a shoestring budget, making do or going without, pulling extra shifts at Cuppa Josie's and selling her restored furniture. And she resented him for what he did.

But she managed to pay everything off herself, despite Mama's repeated offers of help. The day she wrote the last check to clear his financial destruction was the same day she filed paperwork to revert to her maiden name. She didn't want to be Agnes Levine any longer. She needed to find freedom to live again.

Now he just gave her an extravagant ticket to freedom. She had more than enough for car repairs and to increase her down payment on Clarence and Eliza's cottage.

"Thank you, Bobby." She still couldn't believe it.

"No need to thank me."

"You could have mailed the check with a note."

"No, I needed to man up and take responsibility for what I did. I needed to apologize face-to-face."

This was not the man she had married.

Tears warmed her eyes, but this time she wasn't angry or resentful. This time she felt something unexpected. Something almost foreign.

She was…proud of Bobby. For growing up and owning up to his mistakes…something she wanted so long ago.

Apparently God answered her prayers in His timing, rather than hers.

Bobby glanced at his watch. "I guess I should hit the road. Wendy's waiting for me."

"I always wondered what I'd do if I saw you again—the words I'd say. When you asked if you could meet, I realized now was my chance to say all of those things that have been building through the years. You hurt me badly, Bobby. There were days I didn't think I would recover, but I did. These past five years have made me stronger and more reliant on God. For those, I am thankful." She swallowed and blinked back wetness. "Thank you for owning up to the past. I appreciate it more than you know. It gave me courage to take some steps forward. I forgive you, Bobby, and I wish you and Wendy all the happiness with your baby."

Bobby looked at her with overly bright eyes. "Thanks, Agnes. It means a lot."

"If you hurt your wife or that child in any way, I'll hunt you down. That's not a threat, but a promise. Be the man you claim to be."

"Agnes, the one thing I always counted on were your promises. The man you knew no longer exists. With God's help, I will honor my family the way they deserve. I'm just sorry I couldn't be the man you deserved."

"Like you said—that's the past. Move forward."

"You, too, Agnes. I hope this can bring you closure to face your future with someone who will love you the way you deserve."

Bobby was right—his apology did give her closure, but the one person who held her heart didn't want it anymore. That was the closure she truly needed to live again.

Chapter Seventeen

The house was almost unrecognizable from the afternoon in May when she'd come to see it with Ian.

With its white walls and seagrass-green trim and doeskin-colored furniture, the living room offered a welcoming atmosphere.

Standing in the corner, she zoomed in and snapped a photo of the mantel that had been sanded and stained deep ebony. And took another of Pete's painting hanging above the fireplace—the one Agnes had seen at the cabin of two sets of hands holding a butterfly. The word *Freedom* had been painted across the bottom.

Freedom. Exactly what this house offered.

Freedom from the past. Freedom for a new future.

When Ian asked for her help in May, she didn't think she could handle being in this house again. But she had pushed past her own fears in order to help those she loved bring peace and second chances to other families like theirs.

She trailed a hand on the small reading table in the corner. She had salvaged the table from someone's curbside trash pile, sanded it and repainted it with oatmeal-colored chalk paint. With the potted ivy sitting on top and trailing down the side, it was the perfect welcoming touch that begged a reader to curl up in the pin-striped club chair with a good book.

Even though the house was almost complete, her work didn't have to end. Sure, she wouldn't have walls to paint or floors to sand, but Charlotte offered her a chance for something more. Something she wasn't sure she could give.

After today's lunch rush died down, Charlotte stopped by Cuppa Josie's and asked Agnes to consider being part of the Agape House leadership team.

The offer surprised her so much that her tongue rolled up inside her mouth and refused to work.

When she did manage to spit out her words, she assured Charlotte she wasn't right for the job. Charlotte disagreed and asked her to reconsider. She promised to do just that, but what was there to say?

She wasn't worthy of being a leader to these women.

Even Ian had given up on her.

Oh, and how she missed him.

Had it really been two weeks since she last saw him? They'd never gone that long without talking.

Her heart ached to hear his laugh, to see his smile, to be near him.

But he didn't want her anymore. She wasn't worth it.

She had warned Ian they were better off as friends because if something happened, then she wouldn't have their friendship either, but he'd told her to trust him. Well, look how well that turned out.

Tears warmed her eyes, but she pressed a hand to her face. She was not going to spend years crying over another man.

She had work to do.

She had to be her own dragon slayer since no one else seemed to be up to the task.

With quivering legs, Agnes headed for the stairs.

She had come in the back door, so she hadn't seen the staircase until now.

The beauty of its restoration snatched her breath out of her throat.

The banister and stair treads had been sanded and stained deep ebony, bringing out a subtle gleam in the wood, and the risers had been painted milky-white.

The front door opened, and whistling filled the silent rooms.

Pete ambled into the living room, still whistling, saw her, then stopped. "Agnes Joy, I didn't realize you were here."

"I was…admiring the staircase. It's beautiful."

"Ian's work. After the tree took out part of the garage and rooms upstairs, he insisted he be the one to reclaim the stairs."

She smoothed her hand over the gleaming banister, down each glossy spindle. A spark of hope flooded her soul.

Had he done this for her?

She stared up the flight of stairs. Instead of being haunted by fears and ghosts from her past, light filled her heart.

"Pete, I need to go upstairs."

"Sure thing. Right behind you. I left my toolbox up there."

Time to put the past where it belonged and move forward with her future.

Whatever that might hold.

Okay, God, it's You and me…we can do this. Right?

Over her shoulder, a breeze blew in from the open window, caressing her cheek with its sweet fragrance.

Her heart pounded against her rib cage.

As she put one foot in front of the other, the heaviness she expected to weigh her down lifted. With each step, the hurt ached a little less.

At the top of the steps, she pressed a hand to her beating heart. The memories she had expected to crash over her evaporated.

"Pete, there used to be a room here and a small hallway that lead to a larger bedroom. What happened to those?"

"When the tree fell on the garage, it caused some damage to that area. Charlotte didn't like those rooms anyway—said they were too dark and depressing. Last week Agape House received a huge anonymous donation, and the board agreed to tear down those walls and open up this area."

"What was once filled with darkness is now flooded with light." Agnes murmured those words as a sob gripped her chest.

"Are you okay, Agnes?"

Agnes tried to wipe away the tears trickling down her face, but they wouldn't stop.

"He makes everything beautiful in its time. Pete, that dark, depressing room was the one I shared with Bobby. God used that tree to destroy the last hold to my past. This house has kept me bound to the past—too afraid to move forward for fear of not being worthy." A peace she hadn't felt in a long time settled over her soul.

"God loves you, Agnes. So much. He offers unconditional love and freedom in His promises. He wants to give you the desires of your heart…. You just have to let him."

"How do I do that?"

"By accepting Charlotte's offer of being on the leadership team, for starters.

"What if I'm not good enough? I don't want to disappoint her or let anyone down."

"None of us is good enough, Agnes, but that's the beauty of God's redeeming grace—it's a gift. We have to accept it freely. Then God can restore us into something beautiful. Kind of like the furniture you love to restore. You take other people's junk and transform it into something of value again. God does the same thing."

"I guess I hadn't thought of it like that. You're a wise man, Pete."

"I'm a broken man who's made his share of mistakes, but I serve a loving God and married an incredible woman who puts up with me even when I break her heart."

"Charlotte loves you. You two are great together. I hope to have that someday."

"You can have that now. With Ian."

"Ian doesn't want me. Not anymore." Fresh tears pricked her eyes.

"I'm not sure what happened between you two, but I know Ian loves you with all his heart. He chose you time and time again. And for good reason—you're an amazing woman, Agnes. Stop listening to the lies in your head and start fighting for the truth."

She wanted to lean into Pete's words, to allow them to surround her aching heart and believe she had a future with Ian.

What if she went to him only to learn he truly didn't find her worthy? But what if she didn't? Could she live with herself for just walking away? For being a quitter?

* * *

He should've felt relaxed, but instead edginess nipped at his nerves, leaving him feeling like a caged lion.

At least sitting on the dock allowed him to enjoy the midafternoon sunshine as it bleached the navy lake to pewter. The air over the water cooled his skin and tangled his hair.

He wasn't used to sitting. He needed to do more than pretending to read a book that couldn't hold his interest.

If only he could talk to Red.

But she wasn't answering her phone or responding to his texts.

Not that he blamed her.

He acted like an idiot the last time he saw her.

Mom had said Red had visited in the E.R., but she was gone by the time he woke up.

Thankfully his fall warranted a concussion and nothing more serious. He could handle the headaches. It was the heartache he struggled with.

Footsteps sounded on the other end of the dock. His heartbeat picked up speed, but as he glanced over his shoulder, Mom came toward him wearing white shorts and a flowy blue shirt that billowed behind her like a cape. She carried a couple of water bottles.

He tried not to let disappointment carve out his insides, but he ached for Red.

Sitting on the dock seeped with her essence reminded him of the hours spent talking, laughing and just enjoying each other.

Handing him one of the water bottles, she settled in the yellow chair beside him and sighed. "Ian, I'm about to do something I've never done before."

He turned to look at her.

Lines pinched her mouth. A sure sign she was upset about something.

"What's that?"

"I'm going to break a confidence, but please know I have good reasons for doing so. Call me a meddling mother, but I can't stand seeing you this way." She pulled an envelope out of her shirt pocket and handed it to him.

He took it, recognizing Red's handwriting. "What's this?"

"Read it."

He pulled out a note card with a picture of a cottage near a lake on the front. Opening the card, he read the paragraph:

> *Dear Charlotte,*
> *Thank you for asking me to be a part of the leadership team for Agape House. While I appreciate your confidence in me, I feel I must decline. Those women need strong role models to help them face the challenges ahead.*
> *All my love,*
> *Agnes*

So polite and formal.

"She was our anonymous donor, Ian—the one who donated the ten thousand dollars."

His head jerked toward Mom. "Come again?"

A smile creased her face. "You heard me."

"Where did she get that kind of money?"

"I don't know, but I just got a text from your dad that he's been talking to Agnes. She's been unpacking some emotional baggage." Mom turned her chair in the direction of the sunshine and stretched out her legs.

The thought of Red upset, most likely at him, gripped

his soul. He uncapped his water bottle and took a drink. "Is she okay?"

"I don't know. She's been putting in long hours at Cuppa Josie's now that Josie isn't working. Then she's been working late into the night at Agape House, doing jobs assigned to volunteers." Mom pushed out of the chair and sat on the end of the dock, dipping her toes in the water.

"Why isn't Josie working?"

She shielded her eyes and looked over her shoulder at him. "Honey, these are questions you should be asking Agnes."

"She hasn't answered my calls or responded to my texts."

"Then it sounds like you have a choice to make—sit here and feel sorry for yourself or go after her."

"I'm not feeling sorry for myself." But maybe she was right, since he felt like pouting the way Griffin did when he didn't get his own way.

"Are you sure? If you're not moping on the dock, you're burying yourself in work or staring at the TV in your bedroom."

"I fell off a ladder. The doctor said to take it easy for a couple of weeks." Man, what did a guy have to do for sympathy around here?

Mom pulled her feet out of the water and stood. She tapped him on the chest. "This has nothing to do with your head, but everything to do with your heart. You need to forgive yourself, Ian, and stop trying to carry the world's burdens. I know that you blame yourself for what happened with Zoe, and that's been driving you to help me with Agape House. But you need to remember your sister made her own choice to drink and drive that night."

He kept his gaze focused on her wet footprints on the

wooden dock. "If I'd taken her call, maybe I could have given her a ride home."

"But you don't know that. She got nasty because you refused to let her take Griffin while she was out partying. Why do you keep beating yourself up over not taking that final phone call? If you had allowed her to take Griffin, he might not be with us now. So while Zoe made her choice, yours kept Griffin safe."

"She's my little sister. I promised to protect her." He gripped the arms of the chair, allowing the heated wood to brand his arms.

"Honey, despite your efforts, you couldn't protect her from her own choices. That's not on you. God uses our trials and challenges to refine our faith and to draw us closer to Him. Zoe is at a place in her life where she's leaning on God."

"But now her release is in jeopardy after Evelyn Parnell's letter and the damage to Agape House."

Mom shoved her hands in her back pockets. "I've spoken to Zoe's lawyer. Her hearing will continue as scheduled. Zoe is a model prisoner, so her lawyer is confident she will be released. As far as Agape House goes, our open house has been delayed a week, but we will open next week. Agnes's generous gift helped us to fix the roof in a timely manner. The community has worked around the clock to finish the restoration."

"So I wasn't needed after all." His shoulders slumped as he picked at a loose thread on his shorts. He should have been there, but after the incident with Bobby, the tree and the fall, he couldn't bring himself to return to Agape House.

She cupped his chin and forced him to meet her gaze. "Of course you're needed, Ian. You laid the foundation, but Agape House wasn't meant to be a solo project. It's a community effort. By allowing others to help, they've received their own blessings. Contributions continue to come in. Our operating budget is stabilized. God's got this."

He sighed, suddenly feeling exhausted. He rubbed his forehead. "I know, Mom."

"I need to head over to Agape House." She picked up her unopened water bottle and started to walk past him, but stopped and turned. "Oh, by the way, Clarence and Eliza Higby put their cottage up for sale."

"Why? That was supposed to be Red's."

"There was a Seaver Reality sign in their yard this morning when I did my prayer walk."

"I need to call Alec Seaver." He pushed to his feet.

"Maybe you should talk to Agnes first."

"Yeah. Can I catch a ride to Agape House with you?"

"I don't think that's necessary."

"Why not?"

Mom pointed toward the other end of the dock.

Ian looked up and saw Red walking toward him. Hope buoyed inside him, spreading warmth through his limbs for the first time in days.

He drank in the sight of her crazy hair struggling to stay confined in its ponytail. Paint splattered her orange T-shirt and cutoffs. Dark circles shadowed her eyes. Had she lost weight?

"Well, I'll leave you two alone." Mom gave Agnes a quick hug, whispered something in her ear he didn't quite catch and then hurried back to the house.

"How's it going?" he said. What kind of question was that? He wanted to reach out and crush her to his chest.

"Just dandy. How's the head?"

"It's fine."

"You're too hardheaded for too much damage to happen to it."

"Ouch. You look tired."

"Thanks, just what every woman wants to hear. You really know how to lay on the compliments." The usual spunk in her tone was gone, leaving her sounding vacant.

"I don't mean it like that." He raked a hand through his hair. "I just… Oh, never mind."

She kicked at the boards with the toe of her flip-flops. "I've been putting in long hours at Josie's, then finishing up at Agape House. Since I can't really sleep, I might as well be productive."

"Why can't you sleep?" He reached out and looped a finger around a curl, tucking it behind her ear.

She covered his hand but didn't push it away. "A lot on my mind, I guess."

"I'm sorry, Red." He threaded his fingers through her hair. The vulnerability in her eyes as she looked at him cut him to the core.

"For what?"

"Everything. Possibly being one of the reasons why you can't sleep."

She released his hand and turned, looking out at the water. "You're giving yourself a lot of credit."

"Maybe."

She stared down at her hands, then looked at him with overly bright eyes. "The staircase…Ian, it's beautiful."

"I'm sorry for what happened to you, and I can't erase that. But now maybe you can look at the stairs and see past the pain." He grabbed her hands and laced his fingers with hers. "Agape House is coming back to life because of you, Red. You're the one who has spent hours turning that into a welcoming home for the women, even though tangled memories tried to keep you tied to the past."

"I did what needed to be done."

"Don't sell yourself short—you did way more than that. You're an amazing woman, Red. You faced your fears and helped transform a house of pain into a house of hope."

"I couldn't have done it without your help. Working on Agape House was healing. Now I'm able to move forward."

"Speaking of moving forward, Mom said the cottage is up for sale. I thought you were going to buy it?"

She shrugged. "Agape House can use the money more than I can. For some of those women, it may be their own hope for a future. Mama won't mind if I stay with her for a while longer."

"Where'd the ten grand come from, Red?"

"How'd you know about that?"

"Mom told me, but only me."

"Bobby gave me a check to pay back his gambling debts from when we were married. For the first time in a long time, I didn't have to scrimp to pay for my car repairs. I had plenty for a sizable down payment for the cottage." She pulled her hands away and stood. Crossing her arms, she looked out over the water. "But when the tree caused damage to Agape House, none of that mattered. I donated the money on the condition my name was never mentioned."

"But why?"

She turned around, her eyes sad, causing his chest to constrict. "Because I wanted to help you restore your dream, Ian. Bring your family back together." She dropped her gaze to her feet, her words lowering to almost a whisper. "To prove I was worthy."

He reached for her, wrapping her into the fold of his embrace. Breathing deeply, he inhaled the sweetness of

her shampoo and kissed the top of her head. "You don't
have to prove anything to me. I never meant you were unworthy. I meant that stupid rivalry…like you said—that
wasn't worth my time and energy. I'm sorry my words
hurt you. Nothing will ever keep me from loving you."

She buried her face in the fabric of his T-shirt. "There's
no contest where you're concerned, Ian. What I had with
Bobby is in the past. He's married with a baby on the
way."

"Wait a minute—I thought he said he returned to win
you back."

"He wanted to mess with you."

"What a jerk."

"Maybe, but he's changing. I think Bobby is finally
growing up." She told him about Bobby's sobriety and
acceptance of Christ.

"With a kid on the way, he needs to. Forgive me, Red,
but I have to ask…do you still love him?"

"No, absolutely not. I'm struggling to let go of some
resentment, and it will happen in time."

"Resentment about what?"

"His baby is due around Christmas…the same time
mine was."

Ian stiffened. Ice sliced through his veins. "Wait a
minute. You were…you were pregnant?"

She nodded.

"When?"

"Just before my marriage fell apart for good."

"What happened?"

"I hadn't been feeling well, so I made an appointment
with my doctor and learned I was pregnant. I took the
rest of the day off work and went home, planning to surprise Bobby with dinner. Maybe with a baby on the way,
we could salvage what was left of our marriage. I went

upstairs to change my clothes and found him in our bed with another woman."

"Oh, man."

"I was furious and hurt and just sick about the whole thing. I headed for the stairs. He came after me, grabbed my arm, but I pulled free. I lost my balance and fell. When I woke up in the hospital, I learned I had lost the baby. I spent a month with Memaw in Texas. By the time I came back, he was gone. How could I have been so blind?"

"You fell in love with a guy you thought was going to give you a happily ever after. That's why going upstairs at Agape House had been so tough."

She nodded. "Every time I put my foot on the steps, I relive that fall over and over again."

"Does Bobby know about your miscarriage?"

"Yes. I guess he kind of freaked because there was so much bleeding and he called 911. He apologized over and over, but I couldn't take any more. For ten years, I dealt with his drinking, online gambling and other women— the one I caught him with wasn't the first…. He just managed to get away with the others."

"Why did you wait to tell me this?"

"Because it was complicated. I was struggling with falling in love with you and doing what I felt was best for you."

"How so?"

"There's more, Ian…something I have to tell you."

"You can tell me anything."

"Yes, I know, but this…well…I'll just say it. I love you, Ian. I have for a long time, but I can't give you what you need."

She loved him.

His heart puffed up as if filled with helium. But the

anguish on her face of what she thought he wanted or needed tore at his gut.

"All I need is you, sweetheart."

A tear tipped over her eyelid and streaked down her face. "Because of complications from the fall, the doctors had to do a partial hysterectomy. I can't have children, Ian, and you deserve to have a family."

Ian secured her against the warmth of his chest. "My sweet Agnes Joy Kingsley, I love you. You. Hear me? I'm so sorry you can't have children, but not because of me. I know how much you love them and how good you are with them. That doesn't change how I feel about you. I don't need kids, but I do need you."

"But what if you change your mind?"

"Are you kidding? I've been in love with you since I was fifteen. I've never been more sure of anything in my life. Do you remember the night before you and Bobby got married? You called and asked me to meet you here on the dock?"

She nodded.

"I stood on the end of the dock looking out over the water, then I heard you approach. You wore that white sundress with flowers stitched along the edge of the skirt. Your feet were bare and you had a daisy in your hand. As you walked toward me, you plucked another petal and let it drift onto the water. In my head, I kept praying you were coming to say you chose me."

"I asked you if there was any reason why I shouldn't marry Bobby."

"I wanted to tell you to ditch him and marry me."

"Why couldn't you say it?"

"I don't know, Red. I really don't."

"I was waiting for you to say those words. I was so

ready to call off my wedding and run away with you. But you didn't say anything."

"Sounds like we were both waiting for the other to make the next move, and in the end, neither one of us did anything. We wasted a couple of decades."

"But at least I always had your friendship. Thank you for never abandoning me." Red snuggled against him. As he sat with his arms wrapped around her, silence drifted over them like the gentle waves tagging the bank.

"I will always be here for you, Red. Always. I love you."

Ian released her, but held on to her hands. "You're my best friend, Red, and the love of my life. I can't promise I won't screw up. I can't promise I won't hurt you. But I can promise to love you completely for the rest of my life." Still holding her hands, Ian kneeled in front of her. "Marry me, Red."

She laughed through a sheen of tears. "I love you, Ian. As long as you promise to love me, that's all that matters. I can't wait to be your wife."

Ian rose, took her face in his hands and kissed her.

The prayer of his heart had been answered.

Epilogue

He spent most of his life waiting for this day—to claim Agnes Joy Kingsley as his bride.

The late afternoon sunshine warmed his back as he stood at the end of the dock under the makeshift canopy Mom and Mary had fashioned out of white material, greenery and flowers.

With Nick to his left as his best man and Pastor Nathan to his right, they stood in front of a table adorned with candles. Hurricane lanterns hung from posts Dad had attached to the sides of the dock. Swags of aqua tulle, or whatever that netting material Agnes used, scalloped from post to post and swayed in the gentle breeze.

The wind stirred the carpet of wildflowers he and Griffin had scattered on the dock before their closest family and friends arrived and lined both sides. The petals twirled and drifted across the water, almost as if they seemed to be floating in time to the melody of the music.

He and Red agreed a casual wedding fit them perfectly. He wore khaki shorts and a white untucked button-down shirt, while Nick wore khaki shorts and an aqua shirt.

At Pastor Nathan's nod, Alec Seaver picked up his classical guitar and strummed Pachelbel's *Canon in D.*

Anticipation rippled through Ian's stomach. He clasped his hands in front of him and directed his gaze to the other end of the dock where his bride would come toward him.

His eyes connected with Zoe's as she stood next to their parents and Griffin. She winked. He grinned and winked back. The parole board had deemed Zoe to be a model prisoner, so they'd granted her release.

Hopefully being back in Shelby Lake and settled at Agape House would give her a chance to claim the peace and hope God offered.

A lump jammed his throat as tears pricked the backs of his eyes.

As Red's matron of honor, Josie appeared wearing an aqua sundress with spaghetti straps. She carried a bouquet of white roses tied with white and aqua ribbons. Her hair fell in soft curls around her shoulders. As she walked toward the canopy, her eyes tangled with Nick's. For that moment, no one else existed.

At one time, Ian would have wrestled with envy at the look of love that passed between his friends, but now his heart stirred with excitement because his wife-to-be was about to join him at his side and share vows that promised a lifetime of love and commitment.

A gasp from their family and friends jerked his attention to the end of the dock.

For a second, his heart stopped beating. For a second, he heard nothing. For a second, time froze.

As long as he lived, he'd never be able to erase the vision that awaited him under an arch of greens and flowers.

His heart picked up speed as his breathing hitched in his chest. He pressed a fist to his mouth.

Agnes, a vision of beauty, glided toward him.

Everyone disappeared as his eyes locked with Red's and they were the only two people on the dock.

Her ivory-colored dress held up by spaghetti straps had a draped neckline and curved in all the right places and brushed the middle of her knees.

A gentle breeze whispered through her ginger curls that had been pinned up with flowers. She walked with grace and elegance, and her bouquet of ivory roses and blue Forget-me-nots shook in her hands as she drew closer to him.

His best friend.

His bride.

The love and tenderness that shimmered in her eyes ignited a flame that burned deep inside him. His heart swelled as anticipation flowed through him.

He couldn't help himself—he pressed two fingers to his lips, then turned the pads of his fingers toward her.

She laughed—the sunshine of her smile warmed his soul—and returned the gesture.

Once she reached him, he held out a hand and whispered, "You are beautiful." His voice caught on the last word.

"You make me beautiful." She reached up and thumbed away a tear that rolled down his cheek.

Where was he taking her?

It didn't matter.

She trusted Ian completely.

As she settled in the comfort of his leather passenger seat, fatigue tugged at her bones. The hours of the day drifted away as the setting sun melted across the lake, providing the perfect backdrop for their wedding.

After several hours of celebrating with family and friends in Mama's backyard, Ian and Agnes slipped away to begin their lives as husband and wife.

He had given her free rein over the wedding as long as she allowed him to plan the honeymoon.

Excitement bubbled in her throat as she slipped the eye mask over her face, careful not to disrupt her carefully pinned curls.

"Okay, I'm ready." She turned in his direction, but her line of vision had been blacked out.

Ian backed out of the drive. As he drove down the street and made a couple of turns, she lost all sense of direction. But that didn't matter...she'd go to the ends of the world with him.

She ran her thumb over the wedding band that felt foreign, yet so right on her left hand.

Ian stopped the SUV and shut off the engine. A moment later, he opened her door and took her hand. "Come with me, but be careful as you step down."

"I trust you, Ian."

He brushed a kiss across her lips. "I'm glad."

Pavement gave way to soft earth as grass tickled her toes through her high-heeled sandals.

"Where are you taking me?"

"I'm taking you home."

"Home? Why? I thought you wanted to sneak away."

"Not your mother's...our home."

"Our...home?"

She and Ian had talked about buying a house, but since they married so quickly, they decided to look after they returned from their honeymoon. In the meantime, Mama offered for them to stay with her.

But if Ian went ahead and bought a place without her input…

She couldn't stand it any longer. Without waiting for permission, she slipped the eye mask off her face and looked over her husband's shoulder.

A shudder rose in her chest as she gasped for air. "Oh, Ian…."

Tears filled her eyes and spilled down her cheeks as she walked slowly across the yard and up the steps to the peach-colored cottage with white trim.

On the wide front porch, large ivory ribbons trailed down two identical Amish-made rocking chairs. A card with her name on it rested on one of the chair seats.

She picked it up, recognizing Ian's handwriting and slid out the card.

Red, Robert Browning said it best when he wrote
"Grow old along with me! The best is yet to be…."
All my love, Ian

He joined her on the front porch. "Please tell me you didn't change your mind about wanting the cottage."

She ran her fingers along the house numbers—1030— their new address, over the hanging basket of multicolored petunias, and then placed both hands on his chest. "But how?"

"I have my ways, Mrs. James. You like it?" He cupped his hands over hers.

"Like it? Are you crazy? When I had the opportunity to buy this cottage, I thought it would be the perfect place to call home, but then I realized it wouldn't be the same without you here. That didn't ease the ache, though, when we drove past a few weeks ago and saw the sold sign."

"I said whoever bought it would spend the rest of their lives creating memories here."

"You little sneak! You even handed me a tissue to dry my eyes." She swatted him playfully on the chest. Then she wrapped her arms around his neck as his fingers curved around her waist. "I had peace about letting go of this place, but now you've resurrected that dream for me, Ian. I look forward to spending every day with you."

"You are the light of my heart, Red. I will spend the rest of my life protecting you and slaying any dragons that come your way."

"I don't know what I did to deserve you."

"You showed up. That's all it took." Ian pulled a key out of his front pocket and unlocked the door. Then he slid his arms around Red's shoulders and under her knees, cradling her to his chest. Pushing the door open with his foot, he carried her over the threshold and kissed her soundly before setting her down. "Welcome home, Mrs. James."

"Any place is home when I'm with you, Mr. James."

"You've held the key to my heart for years. Allow me to give you the key to your new home." He opened her hand and pressed a metal object into her palm, then folded her fingers over it. With his arms wrapped around her, he lowered his head and brushed his lips over hers.

She gazed into her new husband's eyes. Her best friend. Her dragon slayer. Her lakeside sweetheart. God's promises made everything beautiful in His own time.

* * * * *

Dear Reader,

In my hometown, a woman had a vision to help paroled females gain a second chance at having the life God intended for them. This woman's vision and obedience to God's calling on her life is changing lives for the better. Agape means unconditional love. No matter what shame we may have, nothing—absolutely nothing—will separate us from the love of God.

When I introduced Agnes in *Lakeside Family,* I didn't expect to tell her story. In fact, she was meant to be Josie's Voice of Truth and to add an element of humor to an otherwise serious plot. Readers asked if they would be able to read her story. As I got to know Agnes more, I realized her sass and Texas charm were covers for the pain that she harbored over her past.

Agnes loves to restore discarded furniture and give those pieces value again. Sort of like what God wants to do with us. We can feel like a throwaway as Agnes did, but we can go to God with our deep wounds and scars. His unconditional love and grace can restore us into something beautiful and of great value.

May you embrace His grace to have the life He's envisioned for you.

I love to hear from my readers, so visit me at www.lisajordanbooks.com or email me at lisa@lisajordanbooks.com!

In His grace,
Lisa Jordan

Questions for Discussion

1. Ian asks Agnes to help his family, but in doing so, she needs to face a painful time in her past. Share how you've had to face your past in order to help someone else.

2. Agnes's dream is to buy the cottage to have a place to call her own. What dream do you have? What have you done to achieve that dream?

3. Agnes struggles with trust issues because of her ex-husband's cheating and gambling. How have your past relationships affected you today? How have you overcome negative emotions?

4. Ian wants to restore his family by helping his mother set up Agape House for women like his sister who will be released from prison and need a support system in order to thrive and have the lives God intended for them. Share how family or friends have supported you through a challenging time.

5. When Agnes visits her old house and tours the kitchen, she compares herself to the yellowed wallpaper, having the feeling of continually holding on, wondering if hope had forgotten her. How have you overcome those same feelings of hopelessness?

6. Ian's father struggles with Agape House because of his past; he believes people don't change. Do you feel people can change, if given the option? Why or why not?

7. Agnes is struggling with her feelings toward Ian. She's afraid of moving beyond friendship into a romantic relationship because if he doesn't want her anymore, then she'll lose his friendship, too. Have you fallen in love with a close friend? How did your relationship work out?

8. Agnes and Ian argue about paint colors. How can colors affect your moods and emotions?

9. Agnes considers herself a throwaway because her ex-husband discarded her, adding to her feelings of being unworthy. Have you felt that way before? How did you overcome it?

10. Josie is Agnes's best friend and speaks truth into her life. Who is your truth speaker?

11. Ian's nephew, Griffin, is in a tough place. What advice would you have for children away from their incarcerated parents?

12. The stairs at Agape House creates anxiety for Agnes due to the tragic event that took place for her. Is there a specific place that evoked a similar reaction in you? How did you overcome it?

13. As Ian and Agnes's romantic relationship progresses, she still struggles with her inability to have children and how it will affect Ian's desire for a family. Have you struggled with being unable to have children? How did you make peace with it?

14. When Agnes's ex-husband comes back to town, Ian struggles with Agnes choosing Bobby over him.

Have you been in a situation where you felt like a second choice? How did you handle it?

15. Agnes sacrificed buying the cottage and donated the money to Agape House. Little did she know Ian bought the cottage as a wedding gift. Share a time when you sacrificed something you wanted, only to receive a greater blessing afterward.

COMING NEXT MONTH FROM
Love Inspired®

Available June 17, 2014

HER MONTANA COWBOY
Big Sky Centennial • by Valerie Hansen

When rodeo cowboy Ryan Travers comes to town, mayor's daughter Julie Shaw can't keep her eyes off him. Amid Jasper Gulch's centennial celebrations, they just may find true love!

THE BACHELOR NEXT DOOR
Castle Falls • by Kathryn Springer

Successful businessman Brendan Kane has made little room in his life for fun. Will his mother's hiring of Lily Michaels to renovate his family home bring him the laughter—and love—he's been missing?

REDEEMING THE RANCHER
Serendipity Sweethearts • by Deb Kastner

City boy Griff Haddon never thought he'd fall for the small town community of Serendipity—especially beautiful rancher Alexis Grainger. If he can forget his past hurts, this may just be his second chance at forever.

SMALL-TOWN HOMECOMING
Moonlight Cove • by Lissa Manley

Musician Curt Graham returns to Moonlight Cove to start a new life. Can beautiful innkeeper Jenna Flaherty see beyond his bad boy past and build a future together?

FOREVER A FAMILY
Rosewood, Texas • by Bonnie K. Winn

Widow Olivia Gray hopes volunteering at Rosewood's veterinary clinic will help her troubled son. But is veterinarian Zeke Harrison also the key to healing her broken heart?

THEIR UNEXPECTED LOVE
Second Time Around • by Kathleen Y'Barbo

Working together on a ministry project, Logan Burkett and spirited Pipa Gallagher clash from the beginning. Will they ever move past their differences and see that sometimes opposites really *do* attract?

LICNM0614